THE TIME THE SILENCE FELL

EDUARD SIMION

CONTENTS

ACKNOWLEDGMENTS

Writing a book has been a goal of mine for a long time before publishing "The Time the Silence Fell," and after putting off my original project, I have finally been able to complete this story with the help of some amazing people.

In no particular order:

Thank you to M for their help with editing, giving me plenty of writing tips and generally putting up with the million annoying questions I sent their way.

Big thanks to my closest friend Cătălina, for her help in writing Nancy and generally supporting and cheering me on all the way through, even during my tougher times.

To my friend, who preferred to remain anonymous, for his help in editing and brainstorming about the story and imagery. Cheers!

To Emmanuel Omenda Jr, who did an amazing job bringing my story to life in the form of the cover art. It's an amazing feeling.

Finally, to my family and all my other friends who cheered me on and without whom I wouldn't be where I am today.

EPISODE 1

CHAPTER 1

In a suburban home in Casper, Wyoming, Mark and Dan, two fourteen-year-olds with a passion for science and video games, were eagerly waiting for their summer holiday to begin. They still had a week left but at this point school was so lax on actual work, with all the end of year shows and ceremonies, they might as well be on break.

These two nerdy teenagers were fighting it out, in the new online battle royale game that had come out that year, with their pals from across the country, in their team of four.

But their big team fight was abruptly interrupted by the scared, high-pitched scream of one of their buddies on the other side of the call followed by the sudden disconnect of their avatar from the game.

Before they even had a chance to react though, the power cut out, on that nice summer afternoon, and Mark and Dan were left speechless.

"Well that's a load of—," Mark interrupted himself as he was about to make a remark on the unfairness of a blackout in the middle of a team-fight between the last two groups, when he realised something was off about the sound of his own voice. They both took off their headphones in frustration.

The clicking and tapping as they removed them and set them on the desk was uncharacteristically loud.

There was an unearthly Silence that had taken over the room. A Silence so overbearing it did not even feel real. It was as if they had been born with a ringing in their ears and it had suddenly stopped. Mark's voice sounded much louder than he would have expected even in his quiet two storey house. His parents were at work and now that the power was out there was not much noise in the house. Still, this felt much too quiet.

"What is going on?" Dan chimed in and heard his own voice have the same impact in this deathly Silence as Mark's.

"What's that buzzing?"

Mark turned his right ear to focus his attention on one of his display cabinets holding some of his many nerdy gadgets, books and other gear. In his upstairs bedroom, on one of the display shelves with glass doors, there sat a piece of science equipment that had been used in the 1800s to make a revolutionary discovery. The Michelson-Morley detector, so named after the two physicists who had worked together to prove the existence of the Luminiferous Aether, was a piece of science equipment that had been a staple of high-school science since the nineteenth century and that Mark had used to win the science fair that year.

As Mark approached the shelf, he was still very confused as to how loud everything seemed. An ambulance could be heard in the distance. A lot of car horns, that shouldn't normally have been so loud in that part of town, were shamelessly being blared just outside, it seemed.

"What is actually going on? This is freaky as hell!" Dan exclaimed, on the verge of a panic attack.

"Take a look at this," Mark beckoned his friend to the shelf while staring intently at the miniature version of the Aether detector.

"What?" said Dan as he untangled the headphone cable from around his legs and clumsily got up from the rotating office chair.

"Look, it's blinking."

"What's blinking? And why are you yelling?"

Dan moved towards the cabinet holding his nose, trying to pop his ears thinking it would help.

"I'm not yelling. Look, it's the detector. It's—" and again, he interrupted himself but this time it was because of a thought he had on what that might mean.

"That's not supposed to blink is it? I thought the light was just for show."

Dan was still trying his best to return his ears to normal, this time with his little finger in his ear.

"Not unless the Aether doesn't exist."

"But they proved it already. Maybe it's broken," Dan said, switching ears and trying to pop the other one.

Mark opened his cabinet and pulled out the detector scratching the wooden shelf, forcefully piercing the Silence. While he moved this clunky piece of kit around, the buzzing glitched on and off and light coming from it flickered. He set it on the bed and the light and the sound stabilised again. He sat beside it and stared, deep in thought.

"See? It's broken," Dan said, mustering just enough attention away from scratching the inside of his ears.

"Umm, no it isn't dipshit. Remember? I followed the instructions," Mark said to him, giving a disapproving look.

"You built it wrong, then."

"I got a prize for it, numbnuts. It's working just fine," Mark replied annoyed.

Dan gave in to the fact that it was very quiet around him apart from, in the distance, the horns, and the siren getting slightly louder by the second.

The teens examined the detector for a few more seconds as they came to terms with the Silence and what that might mean.

Dan spoke up first after their brief, thoughtful pause, having given up trying to fix his hearing for now:

"So, what does it mean?"

"Well—" Mark paused for a bit to formulate his thoughts into a coherent hypothesis, "either the Aether doesn't exist anymore—" he paused, "—or we've stopped moving through it."

"Wouldn't we have been flung out at a million miles an hour if the Earth just 'stopped moving'?" Dan astutely observed, marking his disbelief by using air quotes.

"Maybe we've been slowing down over a long time and we just didn't feel it," Mark argued, feeling his logic crumbling.

The boys sat for another little while, trying to think about why the detector had suddenly stopped doing what it was supposed to do, after which Mark got up from the bed, saying:

"We need to do some experiments. Help me

get it to the garage."

The boys carefully took the detector down the stairs, through the living room and into the messy garage full of tools and storage boxes. There was a big empty space in the middle, though, as Mark's parents were out for most of the day.

They set it down on the workbench while Mark grabbed the remote for the garage door, instructing Dan to fetch the trolley and empty it of tools on a nearby shelf. They wheeled the trolley into the middle of the garage and brought the detector over. Even the slight tap of them setting the detector down on top sounded as if they were slamming it down.

"Alright, what's the plan?" Dan asked Mark who suddenly realised they should be documenting the process as it could turn out to be a big discovery.

While they were setting it up, the ambulance in the distance still continued to get louder and louder, but it was nowhere to be seen. The honking, however, had calmed down. The Silence that pervaded the room turned out to be present everywhere outside as well. The boys both felt like they were in a dream. Walking, fetching and moving things around, Mark and Dan quietly attempted to wake themselves up from this strange feeling in their own way. Thoughts of what this could be were flying through their heads at lightspeed. Was it a natural phenomenon? Was it man-made? Was the Aether really gone?

It turned out it was quite easy for them to think when no outside noise was there to distract them. The only distraction they did face was their focus on figuring out why the Michelson-Morley detector had suddenly stopped detecting. Mark was convinced the detector he had built worked as intended and there was something else going on, but Dan was just playing along for the moment in this dream-like state. Regardless of what was really going on, though, Dan was having fun while Mark remained deeply focused.

The boys had fetched the camera from the master bedroom and had set it up on a tripod close to the exit to the garage, facing inwards. The trolley sat behind them closer to the wall opposite the garage door and the boys faced the camera wearing their science fair lab coats which they found packed away in some boxes in the garage. They decided ahead of time what to say and what the experiment would be, and then pressed the button on the camera remote to start the recording. They lined up to face it and began.

"My name is Mark Daniels..."

"And I am Daniel Simmons..."

And Mark picked up again.

"...and we live in Casper, Wyoming. We have an Aether detector and it is currently showing a negative result, as you can see."

Marks stepped slightly to his right to allow the detector into view of the camera, revealing the light that was supposed to be on only if it did not detect the Aether.

He continued:

"We have devised an experiment to determine whether or not the sudden negative result is due to the fact the Earth has stopped moving through the Aether, or the disappearance of the Aether altogether."

They both walked around to the back of the trolley, Dan following Mark's lead, and they grabbed the handle in preparation.

"On the count of three," Mark said looking at Dan and then turned to the camera to continue, "we will move the trolley at a constant speed to mimic an Aether flow over the device."

"One...

"Two...

"Three..."

They started to push the trolley. The rattle of the small wheels on the smooth concrete floor was as loud as an entire skate park full of people pushing off simultaneously. It did not last long but it forcefully pierced their eardrums. They stopped right in front of the camera, bringing the trolley to a screeching halt.

The boys looked rather disappointed after that brief experiment. The light had stayed on throughout the entire short journey.

"Alright," Mark sighed, "umm, we'll reset and perform the second stage of this experiment."

The two moved the camera around to the back of the trolley, as far back as they could, to get a view of the driveway. Mark then continued with a more hopeful voice after they both wheeled the device back into starting position, close to the camera.

"We have anticipated a possible negative result," he said, looking at Dan for validation. They both smile at each other clumsily and Dan nodded in agreement, "and so we have prepared a second stage. We believe that perhaps a faster speed is needed to trigger the detector." And again he coordinated with Dan through a look and a nod and continued excitedly.

"So, on the count of three we will run with the trolley outside." It was roughly at this point when the ambulance started to get a bit too loud. It sounded as if it was right outside. They continue regardless:

"One...

"Two...

"Three…"

The boys ran with the trolley outside of the garage and onto the driveway coming to a quick stop before reaching the curb. The camera filmed on from behind them. The light had again stayed on throughout the longer trip, unfortunately for the two intrepid scientists.

"Man, that's loud!" Dan said in remark to the ambulance he spotted all the way down the road, about half a mile away. As soon as he said that though, the siren stopped. Dan took his pinkie out of his ear, because there was no longer a need to block the loud sound, and the two walked back into the garage defeated.

They took position back in front of the camera with the trolley behind them to their left and admitted their experiment had yielded a negative result on their hypothesis. They could only conclude that the Aether was gone.

"Or the Earth's been teleported to another dimension," Dan had jokingly remarked before Mark stopped the recording.

CHAPTER 2

A crime scene in a big city like Denver is not a common sight for the average person, but for a detective working with the Denver police department, fieldwork is an inescapable part of the job.

In a relatively quiet supermarket parking lot in Five Points, one of Denver's outlying neighbourhoods, the police had cordoned off the area and were waiting for the Street Crime unit to arrive. They were keeping curious on-lookers from getting too close and contaminating what was now a possible murder scene.

People can get quite loud when arguing with

the police but that was not the only noise dominating the background.

There is always some form of bustle in a large city like this. Be it the chatter on the police radios, the occasional loud driver showing off their modified muffler, or the sheer amount of horns going off in traffic, one cannot escape the loudness of the big city.

Out of a dark silver Ford Crown Victoria that they had parked on the side of the road in front of the crime scene, two men dressed in grey suits stepped out discussing the boxing match of the night before. They seemed to be amicably disagreeing on whether the match had been fixed or not as they approached the yellow tape.

Communication between detectives and officers is notoriously passive-aggressive at the best of times but detectives James Miller and Richard Simmons had quite a good relationship with the officers in Five Points. They flashed their badges when they got to the tape and the senior officer on the scene lifted up the tape to let them through explaining what they had found: inside a parked dark grey Ford Granada MK III, was the body of a young African-American man slumped over in the driver's seat. The police had suspected murder because they had seen some blood on the driver side door at the base of the window and the young man had had a pocket knife in his lap. They had called the detectives as soon as they could and they claimed they hadn't touched anything.

The two detectives approached on opposite sides of the parked car, their footsteps crackling on the loose bits of gravel. They noticed both the front windows were open.

"I'm telling you it was fixed," the younger detective Simmons said to his partner as they both put on their gloves and leaned in to look inside the car through the open front windows without touching anything.

"Yeah, whatever. You keep telling yourself that," said James as he peered inside with the care of the experienced detective that he was. "What do you make of this?" he continued while still visually inspecting every inch of the scene inside the vehicle, trying to come up with an answer himself.

Taking a closer look inside the front and through the closed windows in the back, Richard replied after a second or two, a bit unsure of himself but feigning confidence: "medicine bottle in his hand, baggie on the dash, knife to cut it with. Overdose?" he ended on a rhetorical tone.

Nothing inside the vehicle told any other sort of story. There were some old clothes and food wrappers on the floor in the back, a rectangular wooden box with a tiny light bulb and a speaker on the back seat, and random objects such as pens, unpaid tickets and old straws scattered on the floor in the front.

"What about the blood on the door?" his veteran partner observed in a manner that was clearly meant to test his relatively fresh partner's skills.

"That could be anything." And he listed a couple of plausible reasons as his partner stepped back and lit himself a cigarette.

"He cut himself opening the baggie, the blood is from before, unrelated…" he trails off.

His partner agreed in silence.

Richard looked around the vehicle some more to make sure he had not missed anything. He peered through the back door again getting a better view of the box on the backseat. As he drew the attention of his partner to it, he carefully opened the door to inspect it further.

"Isn't that one of those Mickelson-Morley thingies?" James asked in-between puffs, glancing inside.

"Michelson," his partner corrected him, "yeah. My kid has one of those."

Detective Simmons gently leaned in to grab it and pulled it to the edge of the seat when all of a sudden the light in the corner of it turned on and an extremely loud buzzing started blaring out from the device. He forcefully closed his eyes for a second and backed away a step, his head still in the car.

The buzzing itself was not that loud in actuality, but there was now both a maddening Silence and a constant loud bustle playing in the ears of everyone around, which only served to amplify that normally quiet tone. The confusion as to why, suddenly, every car horn in Denver was being hit at once and also why everyone was yelling in normal conversation did not last long for the two detectives, however, as one of the officers on the perimeter collapsed and everyone was momentarily distracted from the altered sound of everyday life.

They all felt like they were suddenly getting a migraine. Normal sounds had become much louder in the deafening Silence. The people behind the tape started to groan and moan in pain. Some let out piercingly loud screams of horror as some other pedestrians fell to the ground.

"Why is everything suddenly so loud and so quiet at the same time?" James asked in confusion, modulating his voice as he spoke to account for how loud it seemed in his own head. He did not wait for a reply, though. He saw that the other officers were scrambling not knowing what to do, so he took charge of the situation and ordered one of them to call in an ambulance for the collapsed policeman. He had not noticed the others on the ground in the small crowd. No one even mentioned the slight reddish hue the world seemed to have acquired since the Silence had fallen.

In the background, still at the vehicle, detective Simmons was gathering samples for the lab, all the while dealing with the sudden migraine he seemed to be having. *Must be the reason everything seems so red*, he thought.

His partner returned and mentioned having

the same feeling: "everything is loud and obnoxious." Still no mention of the hue change. The noisy distraction was a bit too much to deal with.

After all the samples were collected, Richard suggested they also took the detector in as evidence along with the already bagged relevant items from inside the vehicle.

"I'm not carrying that to the car," James said half-jokingly.

Left to deal with it on his own, but convinced he was right, Richard brought the device over to their car and put it in the back seat. They both drove back to the precinct, their minds torn between contemplating the case or the new state of their reality.

CHAPTER 3

Over the years, a lot of people have observed that babies are extremely sensitive to their environment; some might say too sensitive. Any louder than average noise or sudden movement can set off an unpredictable reaction ranging anywhere from hysterical laughter to incessant crying. While these sensitivities to stimuli are to be expected, some babies seem to be susceptible even to very faint sensory inputs.

On a quiet side street in Denver, on the third floor of an old apartment building, a thirty-two-year-old mother was concerned for her crying baby boy. It was the early afternoon and she took her son to the kitchen and sat down to breastfeed him, but that did not seem to solve the problem. She just could not seem to make the crying go away.

Six-year-old Tommy was worried about his four-month-old baby brother Robbie and asked his mum if everything was alright. She answered that it was, trying to calm both of them down and, putting on a smile, she sent her older son off to play in his room, reassuring him again that his brother would be alright soon.

Melissa went into the bedroom to talk with her husband Matthew about what they should do because she was quite worried.

"Robbie hasn't stopped crying since eleven," she explained while carefully rocking her son gently up and down in her arms, trying to calm him down.

Matt had been working on changing the broken plug beside their bedroom desk. Saturdays are great for doing chores around the house, but nothing goes according to plan when a baby is involved.

"How long is it now, two hours?" Matt softly asked, handily screwing in the last bits.

"I'm worried!" Melissa loudly whispers, trying to keep a calm tone. "I want to take him to the hospital and get him checked out."

"Tell you what," Matt stopped for a second and looked her in the eyes trying to comfort her, "I'm pretty sure it's nothing, but, if it makes you feel better we'll go to the hospital."

They both smiled at each other. She kept on rocking little Robbie while her husband finished up. The baby took a deep breath. The wall socket sparked once violently and Matt fell backwards startled. Little Robbie started crying louder; much louder.

"Well, that clearly didn't work," Matt observed, and without registering that the plug had exploded while the fuse was off, he continued to his wife: "my ears just popped...I think."

His voice was now unsettlingly crisp. At this point Melissa was so concerned for her son that she did not notice how Silent everything was all of a sudden; how even though they should not normally be able to hear the cars outside or the screaming of the neighbours, at a volume no louder than a muffled mumble, it sounded as if all their windows were open and their walls were made of paper.

She brushed the feeling off and said to Matt: "yeah, mine too. Let's go! Grab Tommy!"

As soon as she said her son's name, Matt got up leaving his tools as they were and Tommy called for her with the typical voice of a child who is scared. It had become so Silent that they could hear everything much more clearly. But such a drastic change in environment can make a six-year-old frightened.

"Come on!" his dad beckoned him with a friendly smile as Tommy came out of his room. He got him dressed to head out.

Melissa dressed little diapered Robbie, her and Matt put on shoes, and they headed out.

Things calmed down slightly as they came down the apartment building stairs and they got a chance to notice that things were staying loud on a background of a worrying Silence. Homeless people fighting in a back alley, nowhere to be seen, sounded as if they were just behind them. Cars were honking so loudly that it felt like they had their ears on the hood. Even a dog barking three streets over sounded like it was right next to their head waking them up on a long morning sleeping in.

The sound of the engine of their family car startled all four of them as they put on their seatbelts.

Tommy was afraid but felt safe with his parents. He cared so much about his little brother; he didn't want anything to happen to him. His piercingly loud crying was causing him distress on two fronts: he was anxious about his brother's health and scared of what was happening to his hearing.

Matt was slightly more worried that he could have blown out his ear drum somehow – perhaps the sound of the fuse exploding in his face – whereas Melissa was far too concerned for little Robbie's health to worry herself about something as simple as her ears popping.

"Hush little Robbie," she whispered as they drove off to the hospital with the screeching cacophony of city sounds mixed in with baby cries loudly irritating their ears.

CHAPTER 4

It's hard to get a breather as a nurse in a busy hospital in downtown Denver. St. Joseph wasn't the most central of hospitals, but it did get overwhelming at times for staff there, especially with the new wave of overdoses and junkies coming in with withdrawal symptoms.

In such a place it is quite easy to get burnt out by the constant ringing of telephones, beeping of patients seeking assistance, people arguing, children crying and patients moaning in pain.

Nancy Phillips was trying not to lose her mind doing her morning rounds and tending to patients in ward two. When she finally got to fifty-two-year-old Renfrew Rogers, one of the 'regulars' who had been in a coma for the past three years, she closed the door to his room and started talking to her friend, who was a great listener and never judged her.

"Good morning Mr. Rogers!" she said with her usual ironically joyful tone like she did every time she visited him. She went towards the window opposite the entrance, pulled the curtains to the side and opened it to let some fresh air in. Outside, the relatively calm back parking lot of the hospital almost taunted her stressed out psyche.

"How are we today? Vital signs, normal you say," she continued this one sided conversation as she looked over his chart. "Well that's nice. Me? Oh, to be honest Mr. Rogers, I'm losing my mind today," she said in a slightly passive-aggressive tone and wielding a sarcastic smile, after a brief pause to write down his details on the chart.

"Can you believe how many junkies have come in today with the same god damn symptoms?" she said, ending the sentence with a slightly exasperated tone.

She went towards the chair in Mr. Rogers' room, took a seat and told him: "I'm just gonna rest my eyes if that's alright with you, Mr. Rogers. Thank you..." she ended softly as she almost instantly fell asleep for a good few minutes on the wooden chair in the corner, all the sounds of the hallway and the muffled bustle of the city outside fading away as she slipped into a shallow sleep.

After a short while she got woken up by some random noise. But before she could come completely to, and before taking notice of the prevailing deathly Silence that had encompassed the room, her attention was drawn to Mr. Rogers' bed. His eyes were open and he seemed confused as to why he was in a hospital bed. He looked confusedly at the wires and tubes connected to his body in various places and he gently poked at the small hoses taped to his upper lip in front of his nostrils, trying to make sense of his situation.

Nancy leapt out of the chair and bolted towards the patient gently reassuring him as if by following a script. That's the nice thing about training: even if she is half asleep, a good nurse will always have amazing bedside manners.

She leaned in to check up on him and told him he was alright, and explained that he had been in a coma for the past three years.

"How do you feel Mr. Rogers?" she asked, keeping a smile on her face. This time though the smile was out of genuine happiness. It's rare for someone to wake up after such a long coma. It's a blessing to be there to witness it.

While he gathered his strength to speak, Nancy was beginning to properly wake up. She started having a strange feeling of unease at how loud everything seemed to be behind the door and outside, through the window. As her senses started awakening back up along with her mind, she realised how quiet everything was inside the room. She could not quite explain it but it felt to her as though she had been living with a constant buzzing in her ears for all her life and now it had stopped. Her train of thought got interrupted by the voice of the old man on the bed. He cleared his throat a few times and wondered out loud what was going on with a coarse dehydrated voice.

"Three years," he asked incredulously. "I—" he attempted to continue but he was very weak; his voice hoarse.

"Don't talk. Save your strength. Here, have some water."

Nancy fumbled around the side table loudly and handed Mr Rogers a glass of water with a straw for him to drink out of.

Someone burst into the room interrupting the peaceful exchange between the two.

Another nurse opened the door forcefully, clearly looking for someone or something and closed it back up, frustrated because she could not find it. There was a medical emergency in the room she had come from. In fact, there was a medical emergency in almost every room in the entire hospital.

As the frustrated nurse opened the door and ended the peaceful, quiet moment between Nancy Philips and Renfrew Rogers, the reality of the current situation seeped through the rapidly closing door for a brief second.

At this point Nancy started noticing

something was up; something was off about her reality. Perhaps it was her ears, she thought. Maybe she was still dreaming. She took a moment to figure out what was going on with the enormous quantity of sound entering her ears from everywhere at once.

She looked very confused as she stared at nowhere in particular trying, and succeeding, to make out exactly what was being said outside. The doctors and the other nurses were yelling at each other very loudly; much louder than they normally would be. Or were they?

Many patients seemed to have suddenly become unstable or had gone into cardiac arrest. It was like an epidemic. Many others also seemed to have miraculously recovered. Patients that were being kept under close supervision lest they lose consciousness or worse, die, appeared to have woken up or at least stabilised all of a sudden.

To Nancy, it also seemed as if an eerie dream-like Silence had settled in the room. Now that she had had a chance to properly wake up, she was pretty sure she was not dreaming. She checked on Mr. Rogers with a quick look. He seemed to have fallen back asleep. She could hear his every breath as she focused her attention on his person. She could hear his heartbeat. From outside she heard the loudest siren she had ever heard. It was as if the ambulance was right outside. She walked slowly to the third storey window, every step louder than the one before it. Her attention kept switching from the yelling outside the door, to her seemingly loud footsteps on the tiled floor, to the people outside and their daily conversations.

She got to the window and looked out on this sunny summer day. *It seems grey*, she thought, looking at the cloudless sunny sky and out into the backlot. It felt as if she had been looking outside during a cloudy day; but the sun was shining brightly.

Her eyes adjusted to what she soon realised was a reddish hue. She took a look below and everyone was scrambling; more than usual. As if a surge of medical emergencies had suddenly piled up.

It was all so surreal to her. She felt like she was in a dream but she knew she was awake. She figured something must have been wrong with her hearing. She went back to the bed where Mr. Rogers was sleeping. She checked his vitals again to make sure and she marked down on his chart that he had awakened from his coma. Regardless of whether or not she was dreaming, her mind was telling her she was on duty. She needed to inform his doctor of this new development. She paged the number on the chart for doctor Nowell.

She lingered for a moment and then just thought it would be better to go get him. She approached the door and as she went to open it she bumped into Dr Nowell himself, answering the page.

"Dr Nowell," she said startled, "he's awake!"

Nancy points to Mr. Rogers and the doctor

went over to the chart without saying a word. He looked it over and after putting it back at the foot of the hospital bed, in its small metal container, he headed over to the right side of the patient and checked his pulse and blood pressure on the screen. He then pulled out a pen that doubled as a torch and clicked to light it. He leaned in to check his eyes.

"Mr. Rogers?" he asked in an attempt to wake him up from what looked like shallow sleep.

Dr Nowell was visibly upset by the sound of his own voice. *He looks like he's got a migraine*, Nancy thought.

She got closer to the bed as well, heading to the opposite side. She was ready to assist and learn.

"Mr. Rogers!" the doctor raised his voice, annoying both himself, even more than before, and Nancy who was caught by surprise that time.

After the second time Mr. Rogers did not answer, Dr Nowell pried his eyelids open with the index finger and thumb of his left hand, and with his right hand he shined the light briefly in each of his eyes, moving it left to right, to see how his pupils would react. He was unconscious.

"Nurse, can you start another IV for me?" Dr Nowell asked as he squinted, seemingly in pain. He put his pen in his chest coat pocket and started heading for the door.

Nancy did not dare ask him about anything she saw on his face and headed out to grab a bag of

IV saline solution to hydrate Mr. Rogers.

What is going on today? Dr Nowell thought and headed out of the room giving one last look at the screen for vitals.

EPISODE 2

CHAPTER 5

Casper, like all the other towns and cities in the states around Wyoming, had been slowly descending into chaos. Be it because people were simply getting frustrated with not being able to quite put their finger on what the sudden, weird Silence was all about, or because of all of the medical emergencies that had started happening once the Silence fell, everyone was scrambling like a headless chicken.

Mark and Dan, however, in their quiet suburban home, alone and with no school to worry about, did not realise that the power in the house had come back on for a while.

After their experiment they sat down and

tried to figure out how to proceed. They had been bouncing ideas back and forth between each other. Enthralled by the thought that they could be on the forefront of some major scientific discovery, they had not realised how quickly two hours had gone by. The ambulance that had been parked in front of one of their neighbour's houses was now long gone. The honking in the distance was still there but somehow it was more drowned out. Maybe the drivers had had enough and were now a bit more civilised since the car horns had more of an impact.

Everyone's ears were starting to adjust to the strange Silence. Every now and then a chirp of a close-by bird or the sounds of the teens' own voices after a longer pause would startle them but they had mostly acclimated to their new reality.

Among the things the boys had discussed was the connection between the Silence and their observations about the Aether, along with the hue change that their vision seemed to have acquired. If it was a dream, like their first instinct had told them after the initial power outage, then how could they both be hearing (or not hearing to be more precise) the same things? How could they be experiencing the same dream? At some point, in science, one has to accept some assumptions about the real world, and they had accepted that they were not dreaming. Instead, what felt like a ringing in their ears had gone away and it was somehow related to the alleged disappearance of the Aether. They were still unsure how, though.

Another long pause settled in the garage and it was broken by Dan's crisp-sounding voice:

"Let's just take it apart," he reiterated with a regretful tone. "I mean it's worth it for science, right?"

"Yeah," Mark sighed, "let's just see. I can put it back together, I guess."

The boys got up from their metal chairs that they had pulled into the centre of the garage after their experiment. The creaking of metal rubbing against metal echoed in the empty room. Mark was a bit more reluctant than Dan to demolish his own work, but, with heavy footsteps, they both headed for one of the suspended shelves to look for some tools.

"Got a screwdriver," said Dan after looking on the workbench on the opposite side of the door to the house. The metal and rubber tools sounded like they were right next to their ears.

Mark rifled through some toolboxes and then the tall shelves above a small table and found an adjustable spanner. He played with it as he picked it up, opening and closing it. Even the faint scraping was a high quality bit of sound he could discern on a now Silent background.

They both regrouped around the trolley with the detector in the centre of the garage.

Mark was looking at it as if he was trying to figure out how to open it, clearly stalling. Dan, however, wanted to jump right in.

"Which side comes off first?" he considerately asked, looking around it eager to dissect this relatively simple piece of science equipment.

With another sigh that resonated in the garage, Mark answered him: "Umm, the glass comes off first." Of course he knew how his own creation was disassembled. He was just reluctant to begin.

They unscrewed the four corners and carefully removed the top glass panel; a personal touch by Mark. Inside, a weak laser was shooting a beam of reddish orange light. The beam was then split in the middle into a dark red and a yellow beam towards the left and right and then redirected and recombined opposite the laser where it hit a detector plate connected to a faint LED light, visible from the outside. The slightly dark tinted glass that Mark had found in a scrap yard when he built the detector was hiding the different shades of laser light. Now, with it removed, it was much clearer and as soon as he saw it, Mark's reluctance turned into excitement again. They had made a new discovery.

"Whoa!" Mark exclaimed.

"What?" asked Dan, confused? For him nothing was out of the ordinary with the device. *Blah, blah, blah, laser light hits a thingy, LED's supposed to be off and now it's on,* was his thought process about the whole thing.

"The lights!" Mark said getting visibly excited and almost cracking a smile.

As his friend tried to unscrew the laser from its fitting Dan queried further making a wild guess:

"What about'em? Are they supposed to be different colors from each other?" Much to his surprise, he was right.

Mark finished unscrewing the last bit and, as he took the laser pointer out, replied to Dan:

"Nope, they are not."

Forcefully but without actually breaking anything, he pried out the cheap laser pointer he had got from a local shop. It unhooks with an annoying click and he also removed the battery he had rigged to it with duct tape.

As he moved it around outside of the confines of the box it was meant to spend the rest of its days in, the laser pointer gave off a pretty light show. Pointing it in one direction made the beam appear orange red, the opposite dark red and in between it transitioned as if the laser pointer was gaining or losing power. The shift was not too aggressive but just enough to be noticeable.

Mark swung it around trying to figure out why the colour changed depending on the direction.

"Where'd you get this laser, man?" Dan asked in disbelief.

"It's not the laser that's doing it dummy; it's whatever's causing all of this," he waved both his hands around vaguely. At that point a wave of realisation and excitement hit Mark. "This is a breakthrough, dude!"

They were both silent as Mark spun around on the spot shining the laser beam all around the garage. *The camera!* Mark thought and suddenly stopped facing the tripod. It was off. They had turned it off after they recorded their experiment.

As if reading Mark's mind, Dan rushed behind the camera to turn it on. "The camera," he said, running behind it and hitting the button to start recording.

The moment that button was touched, however, on camera the boys had a loud fit of pain. They both gritted their teeth and groaned, Mark in full view of the camera. He dropped the laser pointer and the battery, breaking them both, and Dan knelt on the floor. They were both stunned for a good few seconds. Their young brains had only just then snapped because of the stress of going through the change of background noise. Maybe they had not notice the pain because they had been too focused on the discovery; or maybe the young ones took longer to be affected so strongly.

"Well, that's gone..." Mark said with a disappointed tone that echoed for too long in the wide garage.

"You can get another one, can't you?" Dan tried to reassure his friend. "Let's go to the junkyard."

"Yeah, I guess...how's the camera?" Mark asked, looking up for a second from his mess on the concrete floor. He saw the red light was on. It had been recording the entire sequence.

"It's good," Dan said in a comforting tone. He then looked to make sure it had indeed been recording, gave it a brief second thought to make sure it was the right thing to do, and turned it off. A lot of the time when it came to decision-making he was unsure of himself. It was even more pronounced when he was around his smarter friend. Unbeknownst to him though, he was getting better at making the right calls.

They looked at the few seconds of footage they thought they had managed to catch of the light show before the unfortunate accident. The sound on the video was just as crisp on the Silent background as real life was. There was nothing there, however. It had been turned on too late. It had only managed to film Mark dropping the laser pointer and battery and the sound of Dan's knees hitting the floor, as well as the conversation they had right after as he was getting up.

After rewatching that scene a few more times to make sure there was nothing useful on the recording, they watched their experiment again. All the data they were left with was what they remembered of the little time they had been able to use the pointer; unless they found the parts to fix it.

A few minutes of rewinds later and the two decided it was time to head out to the junkyard to find spares for Mark's Michelson-Morley detector. They needed to look for another laser pointer and a small remote control battery. Perhaps a portable charger and rechargeable batteries, but that was probably wishful thinking by the boys.

Mark's uncle Steve worked at the local junkyard and he always let the kids in to dig around. 'It's a good outdoorsy activity,' he would always say. 'Gets the boys away from their computers for a change.'

Mark and Dan put some proper shoes on, they closed the old garage door, which was loud enough even without the eerie Silence, grabbed some cash for some snacks and maybe to barter with the Radio Shack guy, locked up and headed out. They had planned to go by Radio Shack just in case they did not find anything useful at the dump.

They grabbed their bikes that they had left out in Mark's front yard after they came back from school, and rode out towards the centre of Casper. The junkyard was on the other side of town, towards the mountains, to the South.

On their way out from their corner of town they went past 'old man Mackey's' place: the nice, lonely old man in the neighbourhood that barely left the house and would always give great candy for Halloween. The ambulance, whose obnoxious siren the two had heard loudly before, from all the way down at Mark's house, was parked just outside. The paramedics were rolling out a stretcher with someone on it. Their face was covered. As they rode past they heard a woman's desperate crying coming from inside the house. It was piercingly loud now that the world had become so Silent.

Before they rode too far away Mark noticed one of the paramedics had some blood coming out of their ears. The woman maintained a strong air of professionalism as the few drops of blood that came out, likely because of the transition between Loud and Silent, had dried out down to her jaw. The only reason he noticed was because she had a very pale complexion and the blood stood out in stark contrast. A thought popped into his head and he checked his own ear. He took his left hand off the handlebars and poked his pinkie finger in his ear as far as he could. He pulled it out and spotted some red on the tip of his freshly cut fingernail. He made a mental note of this and continued riding forward without letting Dan know. He had a feeling Dan was already spooked enough about this whole thing.

They turned right at the end of their long street to go into town.

The rattling of the bike chain was overpowering any other sound that the boys might have been able to hear. As they got closer to the centre, however, there were now a lot of people arguing, more sirens and footsteps on the sidewalk; it all just melded together in a migraine that did not quite hurt but felt very uncomfortable to them.

Dan, who was leading the way on his hand-me-down BMX, hit the brakes suddenly. Mark nearly crashed into him but before he got a chance to question his friend about it Dan asked:

"Do you hear that?"

Mark tried to answer but his "what" elongated into a scream of pain as his ears started ringing. They were ringing with a familiar tone, however. The noise was back. The noise that had been playing in their ears, and the ears of every other creature on Earth since the beginning of life, and that was now only noticeable because it had been gone for a short while, was yet again manifesting in its majestic Loudness; a Loudness that quickly faded away into normality. Everything was back to normal; for now...

The boys were stunned for a while and felt as though they had just woken up from a very vivid dream. Their bikes quickly ended up on the ground and they were struggling to keep their balance shambling away. They sat down on the curb to process what had just happened. Had it all been a dream? Was reality this noisy?

It was hard to tell but the guys felt as though the overwhelming buzzing actually made the world quieter somehow; definitely more bearable.

CHAPTER 6

Detective Simmons was weaving between the desks of the bustling office floor of the precinct eager to return to his partner. With the Aether noise back, the constant chattering of people and the sound of phones ringing one after another, along with the loud city outside through the open windows, were all manageable sounds; routine even.

Now much more able to think, Richard approached his partner who was hard at work watching a family video his son had sent him. He did not fear anyone calling him out on it. No one ever did.

"I've spoken to the guys in forensics,"

Richard begins, "and they say they heard it too."

"What did they hear?" James asked, still smiling after watching the funny video. He looked over at his partner.

"You know," Richard paused for a brief second, "the Silence."

"They heard—" *pause for comedic effect,* "—the Silence," he raised his eyebrows as far as he could and smiled sarcastically. The only thing that would have made James's expression more comical was if he could control each eyebrow individually.

"You know what I mean. It's freaky, right?"

"Right. The results?"

Slightly bothered, but not surprised by his partner's rudeness, Richard softly scoffed and answered him nonetheless:

"Yeah, it was HIS blood, HIS DNA et cetera et cetera, no other traces of DNA other than the victim's..." he quoted the report that he had been holding as he was walking up.

"Interesting," James remarked as he turned back around to his desk, minimising the video. "What about the autopsy," he continued with a more serious tone this time.

"Overdose, like I said," he grinned, proud of his initial assessment at the scene earlier that day.

"And the blood on the door?"

"His, apparently. Must've cut himself

opening the bag." *Like I said,* he thought.

"Must've," Detective Miller mumbled as he opened up a text document and began to correct a few things he had written previously in a file named simply 'notes.'

His partner continued: "he did have a fresh cut on his left hand."

"Right." James mumbled again just before saving his work and turning back around in his office chair to face his partner.

He checked his watch and got up from his seat telling Richard to get the car ready and wait for him in the lot. He took a trip to the bathroom putting his thoughts in order. Afterwards he went back to his desk to put his computer in sleep mode and then headed to the lift.

Detective Simmons headed straight down and pulled the car around to the lift in the underground parking lot to wait for his partner. He got a bit lost in his own thoughts. It was not a murder, but still he could not help but think much too deeply about that dead junkie he had seen. He had tried to ignore him as best he could at the scene but the image was burnt into his mind.

James startled him when he opened the car door and got in the front seat next to him. Without saying a word to each other Richard drove out of the parking lot and onto the busy street.

The ride into town had the two silent,

thinking about the case and everything else involved. What had been that strange feeling that was now gone. Everyone seemed to have felt it; heard it. Was this really what the world sounded like? All that buzzing, all that Loudness? Should they even care? Was this enough to warrant them being distracted from their case? All valid questions; all without an answer for now.

Time flies when one is lost in one's thoughts, driving on autopilot. Even sitting in traffic is but a distant memory, ever-present for any driver in a big city. No one day is any different from any other.

In an almost identical fashion to the first time they had stopped here, their silver sedan pulled up and the two detectives stepped out and headed towards the location where the victim's car had been. The towing company had done a splendid job of not contaminating the area as they left. The two crouched straight under the yellow police tape and continued towards the parking space, the location of which was only obvious now because of the chalk marks left on the tarmac by the police.

James stopped some distance back to get a panoramic view of the now empty lot. He glared from left to right to see if there was some clue that told him where to start that time around. Nothing jumped out at him. His partner on the other hand stopped and wondered. It was his first case involving a dead victim. Overdose or not, he had not seen a dead body before. Not like this. Not at his job. A stranger on the street whose life he now had to judge impartially. They spent some time not saying anything to each other. Richard stood around uncomfortably, hands in his pockets, while James seemed right at home.

Genuinely curious as to what his partner was thinking and slightly confused as to what they were doing there, Richard broke the silence:

"So? What are we looking for?"

"Something we've missed," answered his partner. "Not sure what though."

"Do we just…" he paused and looks around, "look around?"

I guess we're looking around, he thought when his partner didn't answer.

James was unusually quiet. The only times Richard had seen him stay this quiet was when he was concerned. He was never been able to quite get a full read on him. Every time he thought he could predict what he was going to do or how he was going to react, James would do something out of the ordinary. Fact which would turn all of his partner's ideas about him on their heads. Mysterious? Sure. Annoying? Definitely. He looked around as well.

"I don't think we missed anything," Richard said to cut through the silence.

"No, I don't think so either," James muttered inaudibly. "We're missing something," he continued, this time addressing his partner. "A bit of information. He didn't have enough in there to OD."

"Yeah, you're right" Richard said, remembering his own hypothesis. While he was handing all of the bits of evidence in and during some of the tests which he had attended, he had thought the same thing. "He could have only had about fifty milligrams in that bag."

"I think he was mixing," James continued.

"What with? He didn't have anything else on him."

"He was meeting someone," James said looking around some more. "He must've got impatient and just did them right here and there."

"In broad daylight?"

"Maybe not. The shop opens late in the morning and if people didn't report it thinking it was someone sleeping in their car…"

It all fits together, Richard thought.

"But how do we know for sure?" he asked James.

"Come on!" James said, reaching out gesturing for his partner to hand him the keys and heading towards the car. "Let's pay a visit to one of my informants."

"Which one?" asked Richard, curious.

"You don't know him."

"Is he that bad?" He asked as they were just about to get in the car.

His partner paused for the briefest of seconds and answered: "worse."

They got in and headed out to the outskirts of Denver. The drive was still quiet but this time it did not feel as short. In fact, as far as James was concerned, getting there could not have lasted long enough if it had taken forever.

CHAPTER 7

In a rundown, dusty laboratory at the base of a mountain, a lone astrophysicist was struggling to continue his life's work. Some time before, Dr Leopold Smith had managed to convince the United States Government to fund his research.

The man had had an idea. An idea that would expand humanity's knowledge of the Aether, which had not been enough to get him the support he needed. What had got their attention, however, had been the promise of potential invisibility. His great pitch and intentional embellishment of the truth had managed to get him the funding he needed to assemble a small team.

A couple of years in, however, when the number of results had started dwindling, so had the monthly pay checks. One by one, his fellow scientists had understandably started leaving. They had all had bills to pay, after all. He had not been upset at his colleagues leaving, but more at himself for not being able to provide the results that would keep them here.

He, however, had stayed and had promised himself he would finish his research. Little did he know that just as all hope seemed lost, a breakthrough would happen. Perhaps it is humanity's way to progress. Perhaps that time it was some other power at work.

In any case, now, a full five months after his last colleague had left, but almost a year after he had lost all funding, he was confident he could power the device on. His aim in the beginning had been to locally 'turn off' the Aether, so to speak.

Dr Smith had been hard at work not perfecting his calculations, adjusting or calibrating the device, but getting his timings right. He needed to operate four consoles simultaneously in order to allow the device, which he had given up on naming at that point, to activate and run for any amount of time. He had set up a lot of precise timers to allow himself to only focus on the one important middle console; the one with all of the useful data which would then allow him to switch seats and adjust certain parameters on the other consoles in time.

This clever piece of technology, three years

in the making, stood encased in glass and looked as if it had been hastily put together. A steampunk-esque mess of cables, wires, tubes and valves to complete the look. Three sets of consoles adorned the rest of the large chamber, one in the middle and the others on either side between the device and the exit. They looked neat from the front but around the back they were an even bigger mess of thick cables all connecting to the device through holes in the glass enclosure or the floor. There was only one chair left now: Dr Smith's personal desk chair which he would use to wheel around between the consoles.

Not long now, he thought. He had been working tirelessly for the past week on getting all the timings right. He dialled in the last timer and on he went. *For science!*

As with many experiments, based on the amount of assumptions that Leopold had had to make in order to get this device operational, there were bound to be slight errors in calibration.

...

The doctor exclaimed in pain as he woke up and realised he was on the floor. The chair he had tried to catch on his way down was now laying flat on its back a few feet away. He grabbed onto the console and lifted himself up. *What just happened?* he thought as he tried to make sense of everything by looking at the only thing he knew could give him a true picture of the world.

The data did not lie. He had activated the

device and it worked as intended: it nullified the Aether around it. Unfortunately that had had some interesting consequences. For one, it gave the doctor a splitting headache. His ears were bleeding and it appeared that it worked much more efficiently than he had expected. The originally intended local effect had apparently encompassed a larger area than predicted: all of the states around Wyoming to be precise.

Once he was confident that all his senses were fully functioning again he paused for a second to take it all in. *It's so...quiet.*

He uttered one vowel, like what children do when they go to the doctor's office to get their throats checked out. He was baffled. The Silence was overwhelming. "Wow" was the only other thing that echoed in the warehouse he had turned into a lab, before going back to reading the screens. *All this data to analyse! It all worked perfectly!*

I didn't know we had sensor towers that far out, he thought, looking at the map. "Wait!" he wondered aloud, his voice viciously cutting through the unearthly Silence once more. *Only on ten percent power?* He looked at the device through the glass above his console. "Oh no..."

He frantically punched in some commands on the centre console and turned off the device. The ensuing Loudness was overwhelming but somehow comforting. His ears rang and his headache ceased leaving only aftershocks. The device silently winded down and he let out a sigh of relief. The chair was still on the floor. He wanted to sit down but he had to bend over to grab it. Another sigh was all he could muster.

Fear is a powerful feeling. Sometimes even if you expect something to happen; not that anyone ever really expects the army to knock down the door to their lab and point automatic rifles at them. The adrenaline rushed into Leopold's every muscle and all he could think was: *I need to follow orders or I'm going to die.*

Unbeknownst to him, the doctor had been out cold for the better part of three hours before turning the device off. Plenty of time for chaos to ensue in the surrounding area.

In a flash, soldiers loudly flooded into the room and ordered the professor to get down on the ground. As if on autopilot, the professor quickly found himself lying down and sporting a brand new set of nylon handcuffs.

"Area secure," said a voice under a mask to what was clearly a commanding officer, after the stomping stopped around the lab.

The CO pulled down his green balaclava and headed towards the professor who tried to stare up at the armed man coming towards him.

"Get him up, please," the colonel ordered the man who had put on the cuffs.

They helped the doctor up on his feet and onto his office chair that the soldiers kindly righted for him, and was promptly interrogated.

"What's going on?" he managed to mumble before the colonel got a chance to begin his line of questioning.

"I'm Colonel Danski with the U.S. Army," he introduced himself in a serious tone. "What are you doing in this lab?"

The colonel crossed his arms and took an imposing stance, feet spread apart, looking down at the doctor.

"Research," answered Dr Smith and boldly continued with his own question: "what are YOU doing here scaring the crap out of a poor physicist?"

"We got reports of unauthorised activation of the Leopold device. Do you know what you're dealing with here doc?" the colonel asked, completely unaware of who the man he was interrogating was or what the creator of the "Leopold device," as he called it, looked like.

"The Leopold— I'M Leopold!" The doctor raised his voice, starting to feel like he was being mocked. "Doctor Leopold Smith? That's me! What are you doing in MY lab?"

One of the other soldiers had found the doctor's bag and searched it for any form of identification while this was happening. He returned with the doctor's driving licence and handed it to the colonel.

In a sudden change of behaviour from

himself and all of his men without even saying a word about it, Colonel Danski instructed the man that had cuffed the doctor to release him. After his binds were cut and his licence handed to him, the colonel continued the discussion.

"You need to come with us," he said as he gestured to his men to collect the doctor's belongings and any laptops, tablets, or machinery they could carry, with a tone that now seemed more polite and respectful than before.

The doctor rubbed his aching wrists and asked in confusion, "come with you? What is this? What's going on? Where are we going? Hey!" he yelled at the soldiers taking his things, "be careful! That's my life's work."

A look and a nod was all the soldier gave back and he was visibly more careful now about handling the laptop he was bagging.

"We'll explain on the way," the colonel said to him, facing away and walking outside the lab.

The professor followed, still rubbing his wrists thinking they might have tightened those cuffs a bit too hard. He stepped out of his lab into the bright outside. The lab was rather dark comparatively. He squinted and eventually he could make out a couple of tan Humvees parked on the side of the road just outside the metal fence gate. The colonel walked towards the closest one and stopped to open the back door for him.

The vehicle was bare-bones inside. It had

been stripped and modified for the army so comfort was not something one could expect when riding in an army Hummer. He got in, nonetheless, and the colonel stepped up to the passenger side door and got in front.

The colonel did not want to reveal too much information before he received direct permission to do so from his superior officer, but he felt obliged to. He had to say something to this man at whom they had pointed their guns and barked orders. The man whose rights they had encroached upon, raiding his laboratory.

"We're going to meet with my CO," he said, forgetting that not many people knew what the initialism meant, but the doctor could deduce from context. "He'll get you up to speed. We need your help, doc," he continued turning to face the doctor in the back seat.

They exchanged looks of understanding and remained silent the whole rough ride back to the base.

The drive there was quiet. Nothing like the Silence of the nullified Aether though. It was unnerving, however, to know what true Silence was and yet not really be able to imagine it. Even if they had felt it. Even if they had... heard it. Experiencing something like that was ear-opening.

It felt like they had only driven for a minute. But they had not. It had been half an hour since they had left the lab in the mountains. The army had set up a base inside an old bunker just outside of Casper, Wyoming. They had been keeping an eye on the old lab at the edge of town. They had not wanted to destroy the original device and all of the data, and kick the professor out. Exactly why they had not tried to convince him to join escaped even the sharpest of minds working on the project. Perhaps the conflict of interest with the colleague who had stolen his work and sold it to the military. Perhaps pride.

But someone had thought, and rightfully so, that they might need the help of the designer himself. A bit of assistance here and there, an anonymous message with some calculations, maybe a voicemail from a strange distorted voice. Things like this happen all the time. The professor had just accepted that he had a secret admirer and helper, and used what little he was given to further his research and finish his own device. However he was not the only one following his designs. Soon, the doctor was to be even more outraged.

CHAPTER 8

There is a very strong bond between a mother and her newborn. It is intangible; inexplicable; but it is real, and every mother feels it.

Little Robbie had calmed down but tears still were still running down his face as his tiny eyes followed his mother's visage around. Melissa was concerned and would not leave until she saw the doctor.

They had been waiting for a long while now, in the loud hospital, even louder with the surrounding Silence that had fallen over Denver; over the hospital. Over everywhere? The people still did not know how far this effect spread.

The Silence had just ended, but the five hours since her little boy had started crying had been agonisingly long for her. Tommy was worried about his brother and about what the Silence was, but he hadn't mentioned the latter to his parents yet. *Was it even real?* he thought. *Was it all in my head? Mom and dad didn't say anything so it must just be me, right?* And he needed to be strong now for his little brother.

Nothing relieves a person's fears like getting to speak with a figure of authority. A nurse finally, after hours of waiting, approached the scared mother and her now calm baby boy.

She introduced herself as Nurse Phillips.

"Come," she said, "the doctor can see you now."

Tommy stayed with his dad who smiled trying to get his son to do the same.

Melissa walked into the office of Dr Nowell, lifting her son so she could get a better grip and followed the doctor's instructions to place him on the exam table.

"What seems to be the problem," he asked her and forced a smile for the sake of the baby who was now almost about to fall asleep. He came over next to the examination bed.

"He just started crying out of nowhere. He wasn't hungry, I don't think he came down with anything, we're very careful not to get him sick..."

She paused. "It's stopped now."

"When did it start?" the doctor asked while gently pressing the stethoscope onto the baby's chest to check his breathing.

"At around eleven o'clock," she answered. "And it got worse around one."

The doctor didn't continue right away. He looked at the floor for a brief moment having had a realisation. He asked: "did it stop about half an hour ago?"

Melissa paused as well before answering when she also got hit with a realisation of her own; that of how long they had waited.

"Umm, yes. Right about when my headache stopped."

"When the Silence stopped…" the doctor added without any further examination of the baby, as if he knew what the problem was, which, to his credit, he had pretty much correctly figured out. He went over to his medicine cabinet and took out a bottle of tablets.

"Cut one of these in quarters and give him ONE quarter, no more," he stressed, "three times a day if he's still in pain. And," he continued as he rifled through his desk to get a piece of paper and started writing something on it, "go to this address and tell them Marc sent you. My…friend," he hesitated, "will give you a pair of headphones. If the Silence comes back, put them on your baby's head."

"Wait," Melissa stopped him, "the Silence... You heard it too?"

The doctor did not seem surprised at this very unique occurrence. He had casually mentioned the Silence as if it were an everyday thing.

"Everyone did. And some people," he explained, "are more sensitive to it than others. And various effects, even opposite sometimes, happen in different people. Some thrive in the Silence and some, like Robbie here, get hurt by it."

How does he know all this, Melissa thought briefly.

"Go home," he attempted to comfort her smiling but this time genuinely, "get your son some rest; and yourself for that matter."

She nodded, carefully picked up her baby boy and headed out. She got back to her husband among the crying voices of people in the emergency room, among the racket of everyday life, with her eyes more open than before but closing fast. She was tired too now. But she would go get her baby protection from this Silence no matter what. No one knew when or if it would be coming back.

The address led them to the other side of Denver in the not-so-great part of town. She did not care though. She wanted Matt to take her there. Another hour or so drive through the busy city with two anxious sons did not sound like the greatest of ideas to her tired mind but it was what she has to do.

They drove in silence, thankful that the littlest one was asleep. The traffic was surprisingly sparse.

Matt parked up in front of the address they were given and checked the number on the home. It matched.

She got out, still holding little Robbie, and stepped towards the door of this run-down, overgrown suburban house. She knocked at the reinforced door and a metal visor slid open violently after a set of heavy footsteps had approached it from inside.

"Who are you," said a hoarse, but not too deep male voice on the other side of the door.

"Marc sent me…" she paused; no response from the man behind the door. "He said you can give me some headphones?" she pleaded.

The man closed the metal visor loudly.

"This ain't Radio Shack, lady," the now muffled voice yelled from behind the door.

"Please!" she screamed.

Little Robbie did not flinch.

"It's for my baby. He was in pain when the Silence came…"

Tears started running down her face.

"Please!" She pleaded again, this time a little softer than before, her voice trembling.

After a few seconds of tension, just before she was just about to leave, the man opened the slit in the door again and pushed out a pair of headphones for her to grab.

Without saying a word he closed it again as soon as she caught them. She told him "Thank you!" and walked away to her car to investigate the headphones as they all started driving home. She put them on her own ears first and pressed the button on the small, black box attached at the end of the wire. It played a sound. A calming sound. She could hear nothing from outside. It was a silence that she was familiar with. *The silence of reality, not that evil thing that happened today*, she thought. "Everything will be alright," she whispered to baby Robbie as she slipped the headphones on her sleeping son's head. They adjusted perfectly. He smiled in his sleep.

CHAPTER 9

A little while after helping out Melissa Clark and little Robbie, Nurse Phillips was called in the research lab. Her pager went off and she almost jumped out of her seat in the cafeteria where she had been waiting to be called for a little under five minutes. Quite a long bit of downtime in a place like this, actually.

She headed over to the other side of the hospital. She looked at the crammed lift and decided it was a better idea to take the stairs to get to the lab. She walked towards the door to the lab down the long corridor, deserted in comparison to the rest of the building, and nodded at the other nurse at the counter who let her in.

"Is there an emergency?" she asked as soon as she opened the door.

"Of sorts," answered doctor Nowell.

A team of two doctors, one other nurse and some lab assistants was investigating the effects of the Silence on the human body. They had got some blood samples from a couple of people admitted to the ER with overdose symptoms, as well as people like Mr Rogers, who had woken up from a coma, seemingly as a result of the manifestation of the Silence. They did not want to jump to any conclusions until they had some definitive results, but so far it seemed that the Silence, or rather the Aether, had a myriad of effects on the human body, besides the constant ringing in everyone's ears that had only really been noticed now because of its absence. These effects were only beginning to show themselves. No one had had any other benchmark before, but the Silence had changed that.

The people that had been admitted because of drug use had shown some strange symptoms while the Silence had been present. Specifically, aggressive behaviour – ostensibly out of nowhere – seemingly triggered by the Silence. Their blood, collected just as they were brought in, had shown great concentrations of diacetylmorphine or diamorphine, more commonly known as heroin. The results pointed to some sort of interaction between the Aether 'noise' (or lack thereof) and the body while under the influence of this and potentially other drugs.

"Can you tell us again about Mr. Rogers?" started Dr Nowell.

"What exactly happened earlier today?" continued Dr Dawkins, the resident specialist on Aether research in connection with human biology.

Confused and surprised by the question, Nancy answered:

"Umm, he woke up from his coma."

"Would you say that it happened right after the…" Dr Dawkins paused, still unsure of the best term to use and also in disbelief of the words he had to use, "Silence fell?"

SHE now felt a bit shy and hesitated before admitting to what had really happened.

"Umm, I can't really say. I… There's no way around this," she smiled awkwardly, "I dozed off and woke up at the same time as him. At first I thought the Silence was just tiredness until things settled down and I looked outside."

"Interesting," Dr Dawkins said as he turned in his chair to take some notes.

They ignored her unprofessional behaviour which gave Nancy a sense of relief.

"We think it may have had some effect on his comatose state," Dr Nowell explained, "and from the sounds of it even on someone sleeping."

"It may just be a coincidence," Dr Dawkins noted. "We won't jump to any conclusions but this is useful data."

"We shouldn't rule anything out, either," Dr Nowell added, and then asked Nancy again: "did you notice anything abnormal about him?"

"Other than him waking up suddenly, no" she answered. "He looked exactly like someone who had been in a coma for three years would: tired and slow to react. I put it all on the sheet," she said, trying to cover for her falling asleep on the job even though no one in the room seemed interested, other than as an intriguing coincidence and possibly new data on the effects of the Silence.

A "hmm" is all that she heard in response.

"Tell me nurse," Dr Dawkins said in conclusion, "you wouldn't happen to have studied the Aether would you?" and he smiled getting up from his chair as if to say that they had finished their questioning and they still did not know anything. Which to be fair was true; they did not have much other than blood tests and MRI scans.

"Actually I did," answers Nancy, surprised, "But I—" she stopped; her last sound, piercingly loud, echoed in her mind. She did not seem to be able to focus as a familiar headache suddenly struck again. Her concentration was broken by a complete lack of auditory input, followed by the loud groans of the doctors who seemed to be having a bit of a stronger response to the Silence that fell again. Buzzing stopped and everyone was again faced with the true sound of reality. As if suddenly, after coming back from a very loud concert with their ears ringing loudly in a silent room, it all stopped and they felt as though they had become deaf.

It felt like an eternity since her last train of thought. The doctors were quick, though, to begin implementing their plan of hooking each other up to all of the scanners available in the lab in order to gather data. But their excitement was short-lived as both their pagers went off simultaneously. Emergencies everywhere in the hospital again.

They all headed up the stairs together, Dr Nowell and Nurse Nancy to one call, and the other two to another, on the same floor. Not a moment too late after the Silence manifested a second time the junkies had gone mad again. Foaming at the mouth and struggling in their beds. Fortunately they had been restrained after the last time when they had nearly scratched out the eyes of one of the nurses.

They were struggling a lot and no one could get close enough to administer a sedative. Doctor Nowell walked into room 305 with a security guard he had grabbed on the way and instructed him to help the others hold the patient down. The nurses helped as much as possible. A quick flick of the syringe with his finger to remove air bubbles and the doctor stepped in and managed to get through. The man slowly stopped struggling, his groans turning into muffled moans, and eventually everyone was able to let go.

Further down in room 309, however, doctor Dawkins had not had the same luck. One of the nurses needed to head over and clean her bite wound. The doctor did not get off easy either. He was kicked in the head because one of the restraints had not been tight enough and the patient's leg had got loose in the commotion. No other serious injuries occurred in the hospital and the nurse would be OK, albeit a bit scared and with a good story to tell. The staff had not found any diseases when they sampled the patient's blood upon admission, but she was getting tested just to be safe.

Things calmed down but stayed Silent. Any one thing was as loud as it could be without the interference from the buzzing in everyone's ears when things were normal. The background was just deathly Silent again. Baby cries were even more piercing, pagers were even harder to miss, headaches were even worse to bear. But for some people things started to get better as soon as the Silence started. Mr Rogers had woken up again and was asking one of the nurses what had been going on. No one could tell him anything. They kept repeating the same words: "it's a miracle. You've been in a coma for years," etc. etc. The man just needed answers but unfortunately, no one really had them...yet.

EPISODE 3

CHAPTER 10

Mark and Dan had been on the side of the road, next to their downed bikes, for a few minutes. They had been trying to come to terms with the reality they actually lived in versus the reality they had thought they knew. Their eyes and ears had been opened to the noisy truth of life.

They had not really spoken since they parked themselves on the sidewalk. They had just been thinking. They were on a mission though, so they needed to press on. Mark got up quickly.

"Come on. Let's go!" he said to his childhood friend.

Dan followed a bit slower, though. They both

picked up their bikes and walked alongside them for a while up the quiet street.

"What was that?" Dan asked, knowing that Mark did not really have the answer either.

"Whatever it was, we need that detector to work to do a few more experiments," Mark answered.

They stayed silent for a while, enjoying the 'peace and quiet' of their loud reality. Cars driving by. A baby crying as its parents were getting it out of the car and into the house. A faint ambulance siren in the distance. The ringing was so embedded in their very being that they did not even notice it now. Even though they knew what it was like to be without it; they had experienced it. It was like knowing what pain was but not being able to imagine it. It was something their brains had evolved to ignore and it was now very easy to forget. True Silence was something that humans did not have the slightest clue, evolutionarily, how to imagine. Like the idea of nothingness, or just how vast the Universe truly is, their conscious minds could only contemplate it, but not mimic the sensation of true Silence.

They decided they were strong enough to ride.

"Race ya!" Mark said with a smile, jumping on the bike and taking an early lead.

"Hey, no fair!" Dan screamed behind him, eagerly joining in and not letting up.

They rode as fast as they could, trying to forget whatever implications they thought all of the events of that day might have had. They raced towards Mark's uncle's shop with one goal in mind: 'to get those parts and do some science.'

Mark, 'the cheater', inevitably beat Dan there, but his friend swore to him he would have his rematch. He still claimed "no fair" and rightly so. They parked their bikes in front of the shop and walked up to the door looking through the window. The sign on the door was flipped to "CLOSED" but the kids knew they were always welcome. They tried the front door and it was unfortunately locked. Mark suggested they head in through the back.

They walked around the shop, past the horrible stench of the bins on the side alleyway, and in through the back gate that Mark knew how to open. Dan followed not far behind.

There were no signs of life inside the shop and the back door was also locked.

"He must be at the yard," Mark suggested.

Out through the back of the shop's rear courtyard, over a pedestrian crossing above the freeway, was the Casper junkyard.

Usually quite busy with trucks coming in and out delivering rubbish from around the area, this time the junkyard seemed dead silent. Not as silent as it could have been though. It was always in the back of the boys' minds: *what if the Silence comes back? Was that a one time, freak accident of nature? Is there any danger? What does it mean?* The only way the teens thought they could get answers was through thorough examination of the event using the now out-of-order Michelson-Morley Aether Detector. They were sure to find something in the main building up ahead, near the entrance to the yard, where Mark's uncle had shown the boys how the workers organised things. What they needed was in one of the lockers in the side room.

The doors were unlocked. Not many people think they can steal much from a junkyard. At worst they would get some homeless people sleeping in, but even then, some of the workers did night shifts sifting through the waste to find useful things to sell, so there was no real danger.

The boys walked in and the place seemed too quiet. *It's usually so busy here,* they thought. As before though, nothing compared to what it could have been. Although now it seemed like a distant dream. The more the boys tried to remember...the more they realised they had forgotten. And they forgot more and more the longer they thought about it. It really was beginning to feel like a distant dream they had just woken up from; but both of them?

The boys made it in and headed to the locker room on the right hand side, at the back of the warehouse.

"Keep an eye out for anything that looks like what we need," Mark instructed his friend.

"Right!"

They rifled through, trying their best not to leave anything out of place; not for fear that they might be discovered but out of respect for the people that had put in the work to sort through tonnes and tonnes of rubbish to get those things in order. They were getting freebies and the least they could do was to be respectful.

They did not seem to be having any luck in finding what they were looking for. The small storage room full of lockers seemed to have everything except what they needed. *We should come back here again,* Mark thought, finding all sorts of trinkets he did not have space to carry. Dan feared he might have missed it.

As they searched through and reached the last lockers, there was a noise outside the room. They had left the door open so they could easily hear what was going on outside. It had sounded like something had fallen over.

Mark gave Dan a look as if to say "be careful," but Dan answered out loud.

"That wasn't me."

They both gave each other a worried look wondering whether or not they were alone. They dropped what they were doing to investigate as soon as they heard a second noise. Someone (or something) was knocking things over just outside. They kept silent as they approached the door to try and peek outside.

Mark slowly leant his head over onto one of the doors to prepare to poke his head out. He very slowly poked one eye out and peered across first.

Nothing. He then turned to look to the right, away from the exit.

A loud hiss gave him a jump scare which made him let out a loud yelp that also scared Dan who jumped and screamed as well. A cat jumped off from the shelf at eye level across the entryway and knocked a bunch of loose things over. The boys both sighed and laughed it off.

"Oh my god my heart is POUNDING!" Dan screamed at Mark. "Don't do that to me man! I'm gonna have a heart attack," and then they both burst out laughing.

"Sorry bro," Mark tried to speak in between laughs.

They both felt like they were finished, at least in this room, and got ready to head out as soon as the fits of laughter stopped. Not one step before crossing the threshold, however and their ears stopped buzzing. The Silence was back, but this time it did not seem to have had the same effect as when it had gone away, getting them disoriented. It was very similar to the first time it had come about, actually. Suddenly, Silence.

Time almost slowed down as they realised what had just occurred and every thought they had had before about this phenomenon comes rushing back in. But in a flash they were scared again. This time, a real threat. A man, frothing at the mouth came rushing in. Mark's reflexes kicked in and he managed to dodge the six foot, blonde, pale, scruffy-looking, rags-wearing man coming at him like he was trying to eat him.

The man crashed into the door and fell to the floor. He was groaning and growling like a wild animal. The boys ran out as soon as they saw the man was out of the way, yelling about five times each while they fled the warehouse: "what the fuck! What the fuck! What the fuck! What the fuck! What the fuuck!"

They kept running across the yard towards the exit and Mark suggested that they not stop. "Just keep running man! Let's get back to the shop!" Good thing too because Dan had almost stopped.

They rushed back across the freeway that seemed uncharacteristically empty compared to previously when they had crossed the other way. *Probably because of the Silence.* They did not stop until they were back at the shop. They closed the gate that led out through the back towards the freeway and looked through the cracks in the wooden planks. They breathed, finally.

"Is he still following us?" asked Dan worriedly.

"I think we're fine," Mark sighed, relieved that the chase was over.

"What was up with that guy?" Dan asked.

"Beats me, man."

Mark paused for some more breaths.

"Do you think..." one more deep breath "it's the

Silence that did that to him?"

A crazy idea for sure. Perhaps unscientific, but the boys had nothing else to go on.

"I mean at this point anything is possible..." Dan answered, clearly just as confused as his friend.

One last deep sigh and Mark got up. They had fallen into a sitting position, leaning on the wall of the shop, as soon as it felt safe to catch their breath.

"Let's go to Radio Shack. I got some cash on me," he said, walking to the gate leading back towards the bikes around the side of the building.

Dan got up as well. They both started to vividly remember the maddening Silence that had fallen again over their town. *Over the country? How far can this nothingness be heard?*

They silently crept towards their bikes getting startled at every bird chirp, every meow or bark, every car passing by, albeit rarely. They could clearly hear cars on the freeway even from there. No more ambulances it seemed, that time.

They jumped on their bikes and with the intense sound of rattling chains they rode towards the Radio Shack across town.

CHAPTER 11

In law enforcement things are not as black and white as some might think. Here and there compromises have to be made; deals with some smaller fish to catch the big ones. Informants are an integral part of a good detective's arsenal, and James Miller was no exception. As much as he hated working with the enemy, it was worth it, as far as his moral compass was concerned, in order to catch the real demons. Many regard this practice as appalling and tainting to an officer's honour. Many more regard it as a necessary evil.

After another drive through the bustling city with the looming knowledge of something more to this world than meets the ears, the two detectives had made it to Lincoln Park. After a little while of weaving in-between the ever-growing amount of graffiti-painted walls of dilapidated flats and the small groups of people standing on the street corners peering at the shiny, not-so-inconspicuous undercover police car driving by, the two partners reached an out-of-the-way cul-de-sac where James pulled in.

"Let me do the talking," he said to his partner after a silent drive during which the elephant in the room had not even been acknowledged, let alone discussed.

Very sceptical but intrigued, Richard complied and did not say a word, even to agree with his partner. They both got out of the car, and walked cautiously but firmly towards one of the doors around the cul-de-sac.

They walked up the path side by side. There was an old, dusty Chevy El Camino in the driveway with a paint job that would have made Picasso proud. As soon as the two reached halfway up the walkway though, their ears stopped ringing again. A familiar Silence fell once more and a sense of urgency struck the two detectives.

No headaches, no blood and no fainting this time. Just... a wave of Silence. They could almost hear people all the way down the road, at the intersection, five hundred feet away. They continued to walk up to the door and detective Miller knocked firmly once, realised how loud it was and for his second and third knocks he toned it down, mainly for his own sake rather than the people inside. They waited for a few seconds while the muffled footsteps approached the door from the other side. Another set of footsteps scrambled upstairs towards a crying baby. A short African-American man cracked open the chain-locked door, looked over the leading detective, paused for a second and asked:

"Whatchu' want?"

His voice seemed to echo in their minds.

"We need to talk," James answered.

The two seemed to know each other well. They gave each other looks that spoke more than words. It felt as though the words were more for ceremony than actually meaningful. They both knew why James was there, and even though they both looked reluctant on the surface to collaborate, they seemed to have the same belief about the necessity of such an unclean alliance.

"Hold on," the man said while closing the door, only to open it again after unlocking it fully. "C'mon." He continued as he moved away from the door and led the two towards the other side of the house and straight into the back yard. Their footsteps on the creaky wooden floor were all they could focus on in this soundless state. In the background the crying baby had calmed down.

"Y'all can't just barge in on a man like that. You gotta call first. They always watchin'. The hood's dangerous."

"It was urgent, Carl. We're solving a case."

"Man, you always solvin' cases." Carl irritatingly joked and smiled, pouring himself a drink from one of the bottles on the back porch tables. The sound of liquor pouring in the glass on top of melted ice cubes felt like it was being played loudly through headphones.

The three sat down.

James nodded his head and replied:

"This one's different. A man died last night."

"So? People die all the time 'round here."

"He OD'd," James explained.

"Man, y'all better make your way to the goddamn point or Imma have to ask y'all to leave."

He took a loud sip from his drink. The ice cubes left over from his previous drink rattled vigorously on the Silent background.

"He was one of yours," James said in a serious, accusatory tone.

Carl paused with his drink up to his mouth and in the Silence they could hear the liquid settling. They could swear they would be able to hear someone think if they tried hard enough. No need to hear Carl's thoughts though as he was clearly apprehensive about the whole thing but played it off as if it were nothing.

He put down his drink having not taken another sip and said "I don't know what y'all talkin' 'bout."

This seemed to be a game the two played: James would ask some things and Carl would answer without answering.

"He had one of those devices," James continued.

"So? I ain't been out last night."

The fact he understood what James meant by "devices" told Richard this Carl person knew exactly what his partner was talking about.

"Someone has. I need to get to the bottom of this. Carl, please."

Carl was starting to let on that something might have been going on with him. He was beginning to feel the effects of a migraine, caused by this second wave of Silence that was washing over Denver. He very casually blinked firmly and said to James:

"Look, there's a guy out over by the old bridge. He seems real interested in this science shit. He's cheap. But people tend to overdo it a lot with his stuff." Carl took a sip of the water over to his left. The detectives looked towards each other as if to agree they had finished.

"Would that be all, de-tec-tives?" Carl emphasised the last word in a derogatory way.

"Thanks Carl," James said, getting up and walking back the way they had come in, their footsteps on the creaky wooden floor resonating throughout the house again. James knew the way out.

"Yeah, you're welcome," Carl whispered into his glass. This time though, James might have actually heard him from across the Silent house.

CHAPTER 12

How hard must it be to wake from a long sleep and think about all of the things you have missed...? Would you ever be the same person? Would the people around you be the same or would they have changed beyond recognition. Three years do not seem like much, but only because they go by so quickly. For a child, three years can seem like a lifetime. For an adult three years might appear to go in a flash but things still happen at a normal rate. Economies change, situations evolve.

Many thoughts were going through Mr. Roger's head while still bedridden. His muscles had begun to atrophy from lack of use. He was waiting for the go-ahead to start physical therapy.

A lot of information had been thrown his way but no one had really taken the time to get to know him and how he was feeling. No one had been by his side when he woke up apart from Nurse Phillips. His wife had passed away years before he even ended up in this coma. He had never managed to have any children and after his wife was diagnosed with cancer it seemed wrong to put adopted children through what he had suffered.

After the last visit from his doctor, when the sound had come back, he started getting this looming feeling. Maybe it was just the buzzing. Or the change. Maybe waking up from a coma just took its toll on the body.

Whatever it was, it started getting him thinking about the project he had been working on when the accident happened.

Renfrew had not given it too much thought when he had woken up and had just chalked it up to coma-sickness, but the Silence he thought he heard was not just a fluke or his ears adjusting.

Nurse Phillips walked into the room while he was deep in thought hours after the Silence had come and gone a second time. She seemed to genuinely care.

"Hi Mr Rogers, how are you today?" she asked, but before he managed to respond she continued to talk over him:

"I'm so sorry. We're trying our best to look after everyone, but today has been… crazy to say the least. I think this Silence incident spooked everyone and it really disrupted everything around the hospital." She sighed and let him talk while she did her usual checks.

"Silence? What are you talking about?"

"When you woke up," she answered, flipping through his chart and occasionally peeking up at him and smiling, trying to comfort him. "I thought it was just my ears adjusting," she explained, "but there was this spooky Silence that fell over the hospital and others heard it too."

She paused for a bit as if allowing Mr Rogers to answer, but she started again before he managed to finish sipping his water and begin a sentence.

"It stopped now but it was… it was crazy scary. I think," she lowered her voice to almost a whisper and leaned in closer to him "it was the thing that woke you up."

Mr Rogers fell silent for a while and seemed very concerned. He was trying to piece together what he thought had happened.

After she finished her checks, Nancy looked over at him and asked concerned:

"What's on your mind?"

"It couldn't be…" he said. He looked at her and tried to explain after she looked a bit confused and intrigued. "I… I was working on a project before my accident. My colleagues and I were working on a way to manipulate the Aether."

Nancy seemed lost at that point, but kept listening to see if she could catch back up, trying to remember what she had learned in high-school physics.

Mr Rogers continued:

"We thought about something like that having some sort of physiological effect on the human body but we had no idea what it could be. We never had any success and the military cut our funding. Did Smith do it? I need to see him." he pleaded to Nancy.

"You are in no condition to go anywhere. We can call whoever you need to come see you but that's it," she affirmed her authority.

"I… Could you call my lab?" he asked. He was very clearly still weak. His voice was trembling.

"We can do that," Nancy helpfully answered. "What's the number and who do I need to speak to?"

Mr. Rogers told her the phone number for his old lab and mentioned the name Leopold Smith.

Nurse Phillips asked him to stay put and drink plenty of water and headed off to ring the lab. She kept getting interrupted, however, by the busy hospital. For a while she could barely find time to even try and remember what she had promised to do for him, but eventually managed to find a second to use the hospital telephone.

She rang the lab a few times but there was no answer. She did not want to give up and return with bad news to her new friend, but had no choice when she got no answer the fifth time she called.

Back in room 301, Mr Rogers was deep in thought again. He was trying to remember the feeling of hearing nothing. An impossible venture.

How could he remember something he had no knowledge had even existed? Something that had come and gone so quickly it was but a momentary speck in the great timeline of evolution that had adapted his ears to be ignorant of the true sound of reality.

He tried his best, but all he was left with was the endless struggle of trying to remember a fleeting dream-like state.

Nancy walked into the room interrupting his futile attempts at remembering. She had a disappointed look on her face that she was unable to hide.

"I'm sorry," she began regretfully. "I couldn't get through. There was no answer; not even an answering machine."

"That's not a good sign," he said, his mind racing, thinking about why Leopold was not the one at the other end of this phenomenon. And if not him, then who?

"I...I can try again later, if you'd like," Nancy tried her best to console him.

He started pondering again for a minute while Nancy shuffled around the hospital room tidying up some more. It was the one thing he had enough energy to do.

A question that should have probably been asked sooner finally came out of Mr Rogers' weary, still dehydrated mouth:

"Which hospital am I in?"

"St. Joseph," Nancy answered.

"That's not in Casper, is it?"

"No, you're in Denver. Where's Casper?"

"Oh dear... Colorado? My lab is in Wyoming. A few hours' drive I guess..."

Nancy took a few seconds to think and said:

"Look, I'm off for the next couple days. I could go and look into it for you."

"You'd do that?" he asked with hopeful eyes.

"Yeah, I've got nothing better to do anyway. A road trip would be fun. I could head there tomorrow morning. Stop by here to get some stuff and then come back and let you know what I find. How's that sound?" she smiled, glad that she could be of help to the bedridden man.

With a big smile of his own he replied:

"That would be amazing, thank you!"

Nancy left Mr Rogers to continue the rest of her shift. She busied herself for the rest of her long day, excited about the prospect of an adventure of this magnitude. She did not know how far this phenomenon stretched. If it was country or world-wide, she thought, she could be getting herself in the middle of a conspiracy, at worst, or a fun mystery at best. She was definitely happy to help the old man, though.

Renfrew used whatever he had left of his energy for the day thinking about the project he had worked on with his old friend Leopold. *Could he have done it by himself? After three years, did he put together another team? But he wasn't there to answer the phone. Surely he didn't go back to the military...*

He tried to focus some more on remembering the Silence. To see if he could imagine again what it sounded like not to have this ringing in his ears. It remained a fleeting feeling. He was so weak that at times he would get so lost in his own thoughts he could not determine whether he was in a dream or not, until another nurse walked in to check up on him and change his sheets.

He got startled by the door every time. And when he was left alone again he would get lost in his own thoughts. He even fell asleep occasionally.

For some reason he did not want to let go of this impossible auditory puzzle, but at least for the rest of day he had to concede. He was much too weak.

Both he and Nancy thought about what they could find if she went to the lab. One of them was hopeful and excited for a little getaway and to help someone in need, but the other not so much, fearing for what this could all mean. A successful project was an interesting and fun idea, but no one answering the phone? *Let's just hope he only switched labs,* he thought as he fell asleep again, this time for the rest of the evening and night.

CHAPTER 13

In an underground bunker below an inconspicuous military base in Casper, an experiment was about to take place. The research done there mirrored that of Dr Leopold Smith. He had begun his project about five years before and with the help of military funding he had got close to a finished prototype for a device capable of manipulating the Aether that permeates the Universe. The United States military had been, and still was, very interested in the potential tactical applications of such a device. A machine capable of manipulating the strength of the Aether field would, in theory, be able to affect the way light behaved; and as everything we see is governed by light, invisibility had been the first tactical option that had sprung into the minds of every army general present at the original pitch meeting.

This is what Dr Smith's team had presented to General Warfield five years prior and what had got him the funding he needed. However, after two years of no tangible results and an accident that had caused one man to lose his life and another to end up in a coma for three years, funding was cut for the project and the result of that was most of the team moving on, leaving only Dr Smith to work on his brain child with his own funding, on his own time.

Little did he know, however, that one of his former colleagues, Dr Richard Kim, had been working in parallel to perfect his own version of this device and had pitched it to the military about a year after the accident. No one really knew how he had managed to convince the general to grant him funding after what had happened but he had, and he started working right away getting a prototype ready within a couple of years. Testing had begun a little over three years after the accident. Coincidentally, Dr Smith was also able to create a working prototype of his own, and have it ready on the same day.

What he had thought was going to be a small test at a low power level with a local effect, unbeknownst to him at the time, was going to be a multi-state event picked up by not only the detection towers built by Dr Kim's team but also the ears and eyes of everyone in the states around Wyoming.

Sure he had managed to turn it off and gather

enough data to be able to make any future experiments much safer, but the cat was out of the bag. As soon as the activation had occurred, a team of armed military personnel had been immediately dispatched to the original lab's location. Dr Kim's team had been able to easily triangulate the position of the device that had caused the Silence and subsequently find Dr Smith's lab still up and running.

On his way to the compound, in the uncomfortable Humvee, a lot of thoughts had gone through Leopold's mind about who had continued his research. And shamelessly using his name for the device. He was outraged. *Heads are going to roll for this,* he thought.

Passing through the main gate into the base, it was not immediately obvious where he was been brought. There was no facility in sight that could potentially house anything like what he had created at his lab. A small, one-storey brick structure, a couple of tents, and some temporary buildings along with an old bunker were the only edifices he could spot. It soon became clear however where the operation was taking place, when, after parking and leaving the vehicles, the colonel led the Dr to the bunker entrance.

Nothing too fancy was required to open the thick, steel blast door, just a fingerprint scan and a five digit security code. The heavy door slowly opened and Dr Smith and Col Danski stepped into an elevator taking them to sub-level five. It was not the longest of journeys, but it felt like they were going down further than just five levels.

After the descent, the doctor was led through a busy underground facility where it seemed everyone was rushing to get somewhere. A woman in a lab coat, holding a stack of papers and folders, bumped into the colonel when they both turned a corner going opposite ways. She apologised and kept rushing to wherever she was headed in a hurry. How she had not drop anything was a mystery to everyone involved.

They reached their destination at the end of the maze of corridors and the colonel told Dr Smith to wait outside. There was no one around he could ask what was going on, but when the door opened he got a glimpse into what looked like a viewing chamber. All he managed to spot was a bunch of uniformed men looking out a window into another room below, presumably the reason why everyone was rushing. Something was about to go down.

A minute or so later the colonel opened the door but that time gestured with his head for the doctor to come in. An older, decorated, uniformed man got up from his seat and introduced himself as general Warfield.

"You're just in time, doctor," he said with a smile.

"In time for what? Leopold asked the moustached man confused. "What's going on here?"

The doctor glanced out through the wide window

overlooking a grand chamber swarming with people in white lab coats. They were all gathered around a cylindrical device in the centre of the room, not unlike the one back at his lab, albeit much bigger and fancier. This one was more neat-looking than his version. No cables or pipes sticking out, no valves or exposed circuitry; just a beautiful piece of tech surrounded by many more consoles in a circle at set intervals.

"We're getting ready to test it."

Are you mad? The doctor thought.

"I heard you've been working on one of these too," the general continued approaching the doctor, both now looking below at the bustle in the main chamber. "We weren't expecting you to activate it," he continued, "but I was assured it wouldn't be a problem. Especially now that you've stopped it."

"Are you insane?" the doctor tactlessly asked, glancing over at the general with a look that matches his outrage. "Do you even know what you're doing? Who's the chief scientist here?"

"Dr Richard Kim," the general replied and Leopold's face turned from disrespectful to shocked. "You worked together on the project didn't you?"

The general's tone was calm and he seemed completely unfazed by Leopold's indignance.

"So all it takes now to get funding is to steal someone else's work?" Leopold confronted the general.

"I'm not sure I understand," the general replied, feigning confusion.

Seeing that the doctor was awaiting an explanation he continued:

"I was assured you had given your consent for this and had stepped down from the project two years ago."

Doctor Leopold's outrage could not be put into words. However, there was not even time for him to express himself as a voice, very familiar to him, began speaking into the intercom from down below:

"One minute to activation! All personnel to their assigned security posts!"

The brief break calmed and focused the doctor's mind. He urged the general to stop the project.

"Nothing will go wrong doc," the general replied, fully confident in the abilities of the science team. "We've been assured by Doctor Kim that there is no risk and the effect will be local."

"With all due respect general," the doctor calmly, but visibly holding back his frustration said, "I don't feel that my former colleague knows what the hell they're doing."

"Sit down, doc," the general said with the same smile he had had since he met Dr Leopold as if everything was coming together perfectly, "enjoy the show."

The voice in the intercom returned to give a

countdown.

"Three…"

No! The doctor thought and started running towards the door.

"Two…"

He opened the door and ran left down the corridor and was about to turn a corner.

"One…"

After turning left again he reached the final door. There was a window looking in. Everyone was staring at the device wearing their protective goggles. He got a final glimpse of it all before the activation.

Deafness and ear ringing. Reality now had a faint orange tint. *Am I dead? Am I deaf?* he asked himself. By the time he was able to recover and look back, a lot of people inside the room he was peering in were on the floor. The team on the other side did not seem to know what to do: help the ones who had collapsed or turn the Leopold Device off.

He tried the door but it was locked from the other side. A pointless and quite dangerous security measure considering the risks. Perhaps more a reflection on the poor choice of location for the device rather than the security of the room. A keypad on the right hand side of the door could have be used to gain entry but that was just more time people trying to help had to waste before being able to do so.

His ears adjusted and if it was somehow possible, it was now even more quiet than before. He slammed his right hand on the thick, double layered security window. Sure, under normal circumstances that would have been a pointless exercise but with it being so Silent, the bang it made was almost deafening. He did it again a couple of times. No one was paying attention to the man behind the fire door.

Idiots, the lot of them! he thought and then turned around to walk back to the room he had stormed out of. He did not spot anyone around, but he could hear people deep inside the facility talking about medical help, even evacuation at some point. There were no alarms. The incident did not appear to cause mass panic or even a slight concern. He approached the room and could hear inside. The clear voice of the general expressed contentment with the results. "Nothing is invisible," he joked, but he seemed to be convinced they were on the right track. Such faith he had in Dr Richard Kim.

"We'll push for more testing," he told the other senior members present. "Let's wait until they get their data and turn this thing off. It's making my ears ring."

"I know it sounds as if you're deaf," the doctor said as he turned the corner, "but are you blind as well?"

The general gave him a confused and a touch frustrated look as Leopold continued:

"Look at those people down there," he yelled in

an authoritative tone and pointed towards the window at the chamber below.

"They're fine," the general said, looking over sceptically, and as if his beliefs were being confirmed by seeing the people that had collapsed getting up. He continued.

"See? I don't know what your problem is with this doc. I thought you'd be more co-operative about this. It's YOUR project."

"That's exactly it!" he yelled again, "it's MY project and I say it's not worth it." A sharp pain struck suddenly inside the doctor's brain but he gritted his teeth for a second and continued. "Shut it down," he said softly but firmly, locking eyes with the general for a brief moment.

"Alright, I've heard enough." The general continued after the staring contest. He looked over at the colonel and ordered him to "escort our friend to one of the 'guest rooms'."

Another sudden burst of pain struck the doctor just as he was about to warn the general he was making a terrible mistake. Unable to finish his sentence he followed col. Danski to a holding cell further into the bunker. There was a made bed, a table and chair, but not much else in this 'guest room.' He did not lock him in but a guard was posted outside. He was only allowed to use the facilities and the mess.

Normally, with the thick walls of the bunker and the ever-present buzzing, one would feel isolated inside such a chamber, but with the Silence that had fallen once again, the doctor could make out people talking from beyond the confines of his prison.

His headache was relatively manageable but he was unsure for how long. He grabbed a tablet from his pocket and swallowed it with the water that he was left in the room.

All he could understand through the walls was that they apparently had shut the device off. But clearly an effect lingered. Reality appeared like a dream again with the dark orange tint, almost red in certain lights, and with the surreal Silence everyone could painfully hear.

It was different this time though. More powerful. Sure, the first time around he had fainted, but he had already been starving (which he still was as he now loudly heard his stomach growling) and he had been so close to his device. It could have even been the shock of it all. But this time there was actual pain inside his skull. A splitting headache that got better, albeit not by much, as he was removed from near their device.

Lying in bed, thinking about the effects of such a rash experiment and the amount of power they must have pumped into the device compared to the one he had used just before coming here, Leopold fell asleep. Without any ringing in his ears, sleeping was easy. The Silence whiffed him away to the land of dreams. The fact that he was tired, hungry and drained of energy also helped.

EPISODE 4

CHAPTER 14

Mark and Dan had been biking for the past ten minutes or so, on the loud streets of Casper, to get to Radio Shack. They could barely think. The sound of the rattling bike chains was incredibly distracting.

They stopped in front of the open Radio Shack with ten minutes to spare before they closed for the day.

"Ugh! Finally!" sighed Dan. "Why is everything so loud!"

"Yeah, isn't it a bit more…" Mark paused for just a second to find the right word, "intense this time?"

"Yeah, I was thinking that too. It's darker too isn't it?"

"Kind of dark orangey," Mark agreed. "Well, more science for us, I guess."

They headed into the shop. The familiar bell that normally did not get noticed that much but nevertheless is hung above every door of every corner store in America was actually deafeningly loud.

"God! Leave it open!" the shopkeeper yelled from the back through an open door behind the counter, his voice piercing the Silence and the teens' ears.

As he came over to the front, Mark grabbed the fire extinguisher next to the door and used it as a doorstop. Dan walked in with a big grin on his face, the first one since they had stopped playing earlier, and headed over to his favourite part of the store to see if they had brought in any new SSDs. He needed one for his computer.

"You got ten minutes," the storekeeper said with a smile but visibly frustrated, because of the splitting headache he was having and the loudness of everything in the shop, including his most silent laptops.

Mark looked around with glee. He was, after all, a boy in a tech shop, and before he managed to say what he had come there to say and get the batteries, he got distracted by a nicer version of what he had built by himself. He slowly walked over to the right side counter.

Behind a window on a shelf lay a newer version of the Aether Detector. This one seemed to have an attachment of some sort. An antenna extended up from the side. It had the same light and small speaker that had been buzzing like mad since the Silence fell and probably had buzzed the first time around as well. The noise however was much, much softer than anything else rattling, ringing or flapping around the shop and so the owner probably did not even bother to switch it off. *It must have a volume switch,* Mark thought. A good feature that, in hindsight, Mark thought, his version should have had, even though there was no way he could have anticipated it being necessary. It also had a headphone jack which seemed very intriguing to him.

"How much is that?" he asked, trying to contain his enthusiasm.

"What's that, the detector? That's twenty-five bucks," the storekeeper answered and headed over to hopefully take it out and make a sale. If only his head did not feel like it was about to burst, he might have actually been happy.

"Wanna have a look at it?"

"Yeah!" Mark said, letting some of his enthusiasm escape in the form of an uncontrollable burst of air from his throat. The beginning of a bit of laughter.

The man opened the glass door to pick the

device up.

"Didn't know it was on," he said softly, putting it on the table. He reached for the switch. Mark noticed right away and told him to leave it on.

"Have you got some headphones so I can test it out?" he asked.

"Sure."

The man shambled back to his original position and dug around under the counter. He found a set of spare earbuds. He brought them around to Mark who promptly plugged them in. He fiddled with the volume button until he could hear clearly. Not hard to do when everything else was so Silent. The racket in the store from all of the devices being on was quickly cancelled out by the design of the in-ear headphones. Mark homed in on what seem to be two signals being picked up.

"Hey kid!" the man yelled, yanking one of Mark's headphones out of his ear startling him. "You want it or not?"

"Yeah, I'll take it."

He pulled out the crumpled notes and handed them over. The shopkeeper struggled to put on a sarcastic but friendly smile.

"Headphones are extra," he said, reaching out to Mark who smiled back, equally ironically.

Mark pulled them out and handed them over. He picked up his unexpected purchase and put it in the box the man handed over after he pocketed the money. After Mark finally managed to find space in the box alongside all of the safety instructions and user guide, Dan came over looking really excited as well.

"Whatchu' got there?"

"Aether detector mk. II" he replied excitedly. "Let's get back. I've got some headphones at home. We might be able to find the source of the Silence."

Dan looked at his friend surprised and impressed.

"Come on," Mark continued.

"See you kids around," they heard from behind them as they stepped out leaving the door open.

They headed to their bikes. Mark strapped the box inside the basket at the front of his bike. *Good enough. I'll hold it if I see it wobble anyway.*

Dan looked at his watch and had a sudden realisation.

"Can we go by my mom's store before we get back? I need to give her the keys."

What? "Why doesn't she have keys?"

"We only have one set and I'm hanging out with you till later."

"Alright."

Makes sense.

Mark gestured for Dan to lead the way. He could almost hear his buddy's neck cracking as he looked down and got on the bike even from where he was. Luckily the boys had a lot of distractions to help, otherwise who knows what effect that might have on their minds. Hearing every one of their bones rubbing against each other, hearing their own heartbeat and if they focused, hearing the heartbeat of the person they were standing next to. It made them painfully aware of their own existence.

The boys biked up further. The loud sound of rattling chains disrupting their thoughts in a sea of Silence, their only companion. Dan suddenly stopped a little while into their trip for seemingly no reason, only staring out in front, his back straight and his left leg propping up the bike. Mark, not expecting his friend to stop like that, thought *what the hell?!* and asked:

"Why are we stopping? We're not there yet, are we?"

After a brief pause, Dan ominously asked without turning around:

"Do you hear that?"

Falling right into Dan's trap, Mark answered with another question:

"Hear what?"

Dan turned around and revealed his enormous 'gotcha' grin:

"Exactly!"

Mark did not take long to figure it all out.

"How long have you been sitting on that?" He said, letting out a sigh of defeat.

With the grin still there and almost letting out a bit of laughter Dan told him:

"Since we left your place."

"Well GG," his buddy said, "you got me."

*So dumb...*he thought, but he was not sure yet if he was frustrated because he had fallen for it or because it was a silly joke. Maybe they needed silly. Another distraction to keep their minds off the looming truth.

But, sometimes the looming truth finds you whether you like it or not and hits you off your bike unexpectedly while you are stopped having a nice chat with your buddy.

In a flash and, somehow in this Silence, without warning, a man rushed Dan on his bike. He came out from a side street frothing at the mouth and screaming his heart out. He pushed Dan off his bike and they both landed on the street in the middle of the lane.

Mark could only scream in fear. He was stunned. *What is happening?* Dan was barely managing to keep the man from eating him alive; his frothing mouth getting closer and closer by the millisecond.

In less than five seconds, the whole thing was

over though. Another man came running out of a shop just next to them and pushed the frothing zombie-man away. The homeless-looking man landed on his back and he tried to get up, each time with weaker and weaker motions until he just stopped yelling; he stopped flailing; he stopped breathing. They were all sure he had stopped breathing. In this Silence they would definitely hear it.

The hero extended his arm out to Dan. He pulled him up and asked:

"Are you boys alright?"

In unison they answered "yeah."

"I've been keeping an eye on that junkie for a while. Wasn't sure what he was gonna do," the man said in genuine fear. "You boys run along now. I'll deal with the cops." He then pulled out his phone and dialled 911.

The boys got on their bikes with the echo of the attacker's screams still in their ears and headed off slowly. Dan looked back for a bit and yelled, not too loudly, "thank you!"

What the hell just happened? They both thought, still trying to come to terms with what had just occurred on their way to Dan's mom's workplace. She was worried when she saw them, especially her baby boy. She was busy though and Dan did not seem like he wanted to talk about it. Perhaps to protect her from the truth.

"I'm fine," he said to her. He gave her a fake smile that she recognised as such, but she trusted that he was going to be alright; for now...She went back to work and the boys biked back to Mark's home in Silence again.

Zombies now?

CHAPTER 15

On the loud streets of Denver, looking out through an orange filter, James and Richard were driving out to the old bridge. One of Denver's oldest neighbourhoods, it was also a place teeming with junkies and a gathering spot for homeless people. The two drove up from the south side and parked some distance away under the freeway.

It seemed like the longer the Silence lasted the more severe James's headache would get. At that point, closing the door was enough to get his ears ringing for a short while. He could swear he heard people chewing. The closest person was about a hundred metres away under the bridge, though.

The second slam of the door from his partner actually seemed less painful to his ears. His body must have been adjusting to it. The quiet ambience in the car with the constant tyre rumble on the asphalt had now suddenly changed to loud unpredictable noises, keeping his body on edge.

"Where do we start?" Richard asked, his voice resonating under the bridge and viciously returning to their ears.

"Can't you hear the beeping?" James replied. "Let's follow that."

Oh yeah, Richard thought, *the thingy beeped last time when it was quiet, like this.*

The faint beep led the two through a crowd of homeless people staring them down as if to scare them away from their territory. An old man in front of his tent, drinking from a bottle inside a brown paper bag, yelled at the two detectives, his words echoing under the freeway:

"What are ya doin' here officer?"

His remark went unanswered. The two were almost immune to any flak being thrown their way from random people on the street. They had heard it all. Now even more so than ever. They had heard the deafening Silence of reality.

They walked further through the tunnel of stares, in the Silence hearing every step the people took to get closer for a better view. Every heavy breath and every puff of smoke loomed over them.

Don't let them see your fear, James mentally signalled to his partner through his stares.

No looks were being exchanged. Richard followed right behind trying not to stare, panic or show any signs that might tip the people off that they had the numbers advantage on the two officers of the law. *It's all about confidence* Richard thought. *Just keep walking.* Even his thoughts sounded like he was speaking to himself.

The beeping got louder with every intense step they took on the old, damaged concrete. They were getting closer. Deeper under the bridge there sat a bigger tent. That was where the source seemed to originate from. As they cautiously approached, the tent opened up. A white man in his twenties stepped out; he clearly did not fit the scenery, wearing clean jeans and a long-sleeved, gray shirt. The two stopped and stared for a brief second. James, the experienced detective that he was, noticed something poking behind the man's back. *Gun*, he thought. He reached very casually to unbutton his jacket with his left hand so he could more easily access his holster, and at the same time got himself ready and signalled his partner of the find with a wave of his other hand.

James barely managed to open his mouth to greet him when the man bolted in the opposite direction, forcefully pushing homeless people to the ground.

Without a moment's thought Richard started sprinting after him. Running was one of his hobbies. *He's got this*, James thought.

His partner on the other hand was taking the smart approach. James may not have had the fitness that Richard did, but he did know Denver. He quickly headed for the car.

The suspect was trying his best to escape. He had put his mind to running and he was not stopping unless he was dead. He glanced back to see he only had to elude the one man. The two were almost equal in their speed and agility. Every barrel that the suspect knocked over, Richard jumped; every corner that he took thinking he was being sneaky, Richard predicted and kept up with him.

The last corner they both turned led them down a long, empty street. Their heavy footsteps echoed loudly in the Silent gangway. It sounded like a crowd of people was running a marathon.

They were both starting to breathe a bit more heavily now. None of them had the upper hand. The man took one last look and was disappointed to see Richard still in pursuit. Turning his head back, however, he got a nasty surprise. He slammed face first in the driver side door of the undercover police sedan of James who stared out the window with a smile.

He had been so focused on escaping he did not even pay any attention to the car approaching. James' car was the only one that was making noise so loudly down the side streets.

In a flash he was on the ground, his weapon was gone, and his hands were cuffed.

Breathing heavily, Richard asked his partner if any of what he had just done had been necessary.

With a smile James informed him: "we've all got our roles to play."

They all got back in the car, each in their designated seat, and headed back to the precinct. The two runners caught their breath and the suspect now had to come up with a plausible story on the way to the interrogation chamber. His heavy breaths slowly started to calm down but his mind was racing faster and faster. He was in deep trouble.

CHAPTER 16

No matter how much of a morning person Nancy was, getting up and ready for work was never as fun for her as being up early on a day off. Fortunately, this was the first of the four off in her 'four on four off' shift.

She would try to do some sort of activity every time she was off work. Something fun, somewhere not near the hospital or even remotely related to what she did every day. It was the only way she had found to keep sane.

This time, she was heading out of Denver to track down whoever might still working, if anyone, at Mr Rogers' old lab in Casper.

It was a few hours' drive north, with or without traffic, so she did not bother herself too much trying to get up early.

When she did get up, her usual morning routine when she was off work kicked in: she turned on the coffee maker, flipped the TV on to the news, and got herself a cup ready for that "sweet sweet go-go juice."

She was awake enough to just pay attention to the anchorwoman. "No news yet about the source of the peculiar Silence that befell Western United States. Reports have come in from Colorado, Wyoming, Utah, Idaho, Montana, South Dakota and Nebraska of this eerie quietness but nothing mentioning a possible cause. Experts claim the colour shift is evidence of a disturbance in the Aether, the medium through which light propagates, but the connection to human hearing is still unknown."

Am I gonna be on the news? Nancy thought. *Not sure how I feel about that.*

The Pavlovian ding from the coffee maker brought a brief glimpse of joy on Nancy's face. The subsequent freshly brewed coffee smell enhanced that and it turned into a genuine feeling of warmth and fuzziness.

Time to enjoy the morning!

It was a wonder newspapers could still exist in a time of news on demand anywhere without the need to flip through giant clunky pages. Nancy enjoyed them though. She did not read through the entire thing, she would just skim the titles and if anything caught her eye she would read the whole article. It was more about the feeling of flipping pages. She had fond memories of reading the newspaper with her dad in the morning. She would feel like a grown-up, as well as have something to talk about with him; and because of her growing up while technology was evolving, she now had the best of both worlds: the nostalgia of reading a newspaper and the convenience of getting her news anytime on her smart device of choice.

The TV was more background noise at this point, but if something interesting did pop up, she could direct her attention in a flash.

Nancy's mind was already racing. It never took her too long to fully wake up. Even the smell of coffee was enough to get her wired up.

She had so many questions. What could she possibly find at the supposedly abandoned lab? What weird experiments were going on? What could be the consequence of everyone hearing this overwhelming Silence? Was that what reality truly sounds like?

It seemed like a distant memory now. She could only remember how she had felt about what she had been hearing, or rather how little she had been hearing. It had been like a disturbing wake-up call to a reality that she had never known existed; like briefly waking up from a dream that had been going on forever. A dream so similar to reality in which the only difference was not realising it was a dream. Now all that was left was falling into a mental vortex when thinking about it, from which the only escape was another sip of flavourful coffee.

The TV had completely faded in the background at that point and the newspaper had not had anything interesting enough to warrant a full article read.

One refreshing cup of coffee later and it was time to get ready for the trip. She was never one to pay too much attention to making a fashion statement: the clothes at the top of the drawer were good enough, and her makeup only took ten minutes because she just wanted to even out her skin. Her usual routine would usually cut it, but now it was time for the big decisions: what to pack? How long would this take? Was this going to be just a day trip? Would she have to spend the night? Important questions to consider, the answers to which took longer to come to her than she was willing to admit.

She decided to pack some clothes, just in case she would have to spend the night. She put them in a plastic bag. She was only taking one new set, not enough to fill even the tiny suitcase she would for weekend getaways. Everything else fit in her purse.

She checked one last time for the must-haves. "Keys, cash, phone," she muttered to herself and then let out a vocalised sigh as she thought about what else she was forgetting. *I must be forgetting something. Check three times*, she thought. It was more of a habit now. Many a time she had had to come back, sometimes from much too far away than she would have liked, because she had left something important behind. She had been burned too many times.

"Card, ok."

She turned off the TV, unplugged the coffee maker, and she was ready to head out.

She grabbed her keys from the bowl on the little table next to the door and headed out.

A wave of invisible cigarette smoke hit her as she stepped out of her small second-storey apartment, something which was not unusual as most neighbours would smoke out in the hall. That did not mean she liked it. She might have been used to it so she was not necessarily surprised, but she always involuntarily lifted up the left side of her upper lip in disgust. Why did SHE have to suffer for other people's addictions? Why did SHE have to put up with others not caring about their own health and wellbeing, she thought.

Nevertheless, she did not despise her neighbours; it was more that she felt sorry for them and those around them.

Out on the gray featureless hallway of this older building, staring out in no particular direction, lit cigarette in hand, sat her next door neighbour crouched down with his back against the cold concrete wall.

Nancy remembered that Jack was quitting.

Lately he would only smoke when he was stressed. She locked her door and opened her mouth, took a breath, ready to ask him how he was doing but a loud crash from inside his apartment interrupted her. It suddenly became clear to her he was having trouble with his girlfriend again. He looked down with a sigh and put out his cigarette on the cold floor, getting up to go inside. Before he turned around to face his door, he glanced over at Nancy and smiled politely. Nancy smiled back, acknowledging the situation and she walked off towards the stairs. On her way down she heard yelling. She tried not to think about it and not to let it affect her mood. *It's none of my business* she told herself.

On her way out of the building she was greeted by the familiar, brisk, polluted air of the city and the sun rays creeping between buildings in that early morning. The loudness and bustle of the outdoors did not seem so overwhelming. In part because she was used to it and because she had never lived outside of a city at all. But also because now she knew what true loudness really was. The stark contrast between the real Silence of the world she had heard the day before and the amplified volume of the loud urban environment had been a real ear-opener for her. Having a new perspective – a true reference frame – on what "Noise" and "Silence" really mean, it was hard for her to feel overwhelmed by a few honking cars or the occasional argument in the street.

Nancy got to her tiny smart car parked right in front of the door to the building. It was so easy to find a parking spot with a car so small she could almost hug it all the way around.

She set off turning on the radio to her favourite station that played nineties classics.

Minutes turned to hours, but she finally managed to get on the interstate and out of Denver. *It should be much quicker to make ground now towards Casper*, she thought full of joy. Her GPS had never failed her and she trusted it completely.

About three hours into her supposed five hour trip, Nancy realised something. While glancing at the dashboard to check her speed she noticed a blinking light. It was the low fuel light and the gauge was all the way to the left past E.

That can't be right, she thought. She had fuelled up the day before...or so she thought. She was unsure now. Obviously she had not.

"Crap..." she muttered with a sigh.

She checked the GPS and it was showing there was a little town coming up. She took the next exit and it was not hard for her to find the gas station just off the side of the interstate.

An overgrown sign that seemed to have been ignored for years read "Chug Chug Gas and Go." Somehow the words had stayed more or less visible.

She pulled up to a pump and shut off her engine; she did not leave the car yet though.

Something was off. It was quiet outside. The more she glanced out the more she noticed. There were no cars driving by, no one on the street or in the gas station; or anywhere at all. It was quiet but not Silent; eerie almost, but not scary. It was the middle of the day. The sun was out and the event was not happening again. It was just...empty.

Well, there's a person at the counter, inside, Nancy thought and stepped out.

She filled up, put the nozzle back and went inside to pay.

She dug around for some cash in her purse while walking inside and lifted her head just as she reached the counter where a bored teenage girl was playing with some coins, looking off into the distance.

Nancy was confused for a second not knowing how to approach her. She began by attempting to get her attention with filler noise.

"Ummm..."

She paused for a bit to check for a reply, or for some sign she was being acknowledged but saw nothing. She continued nonetheless:

"Pump two," she said, raising her pitch as if asking a question.

The girl glanced over lazily at a screen, and in the most tired and monotone voice Nancy had ever heard replied:

"Seventeen twenty-five."

Nancy put a twenty dollar note on the counter and the girl began the slowest return of change Nancy had ever witnessed. It felt like hours waiting for her to open the register and drag the bill on the counter, letting gravity guide her hand in the right tray. Then, she slowly shifted her hand to another tray and picked up two dollar bills only using her fingers to collect them. In the most vicious fight against the weight of her own arm, and with a motion just strong enough to get her hand barely above the counter, the girl dropped the two bills and dragged her hand towards the coin tray to pick up the remaining three quarters. Nancy thought that was going to be it; that she would take the coins, all at once, and place them on the bills to hand them over to her. None of that happened. Instead, the girl picked up each coin individually, and slowly battled her way back and forth against gravity three times, only to finally push the change over, all together towards Nancy and afterwards say, in the same monotone voice as before, "here's your change," while she kept staring diagonally in Nancy's direction, but at the floor behind her.

Nancy picked up her change and slowly backed away, intrigued by this peculiar person, and eventually turned around and went to her car, the bell hanging above the door dinging behind her on her way out.

Well! Nancy thought; *that was certainly AN experience...*

After she took a seat comfortably inside her tiny automobile with her seatbelt on, Nancy was relieved to see people walking around. It must have just been one of those weird moments when no one had been around that area at the time she had driven in.

Everything is fine, her inner voice reassured her.

The nineties classics were back on and the trip was an adventure.

During the rest of her journey Nancy pondered what could possibly have triggered that event, the Silence, what sort of scientific madness could have happened in that lab and what she would find there. It was still up for debate, in Nancy's mind, whether or not she was lucky to get to figure all this out first hand.

She tried her best to understand this event. *Why Silence? Why the weird colour shift? The news mentioned the Aether, but what did sound have to do with it?* Sure it explained the visuals but not the quietness. Maybe she just did not remember enough from her high-school physics class.

Time seemed to fly by. The good music and hard questions, to which she did not have all the answers, had made the last two hours of her trip go by in a flash. Now all that was left was to check out the supposedly abandoned lab.

EPISODE 5

CHAPTER 17

Mark had not managed to get a good rest the night before. His mind had been racing. He could not let go of the questions flying through his head. *What was the Silence all about? Was it a natural event? If not, who or what caused it? What's the connection with sound if the Aether is the thing that's being disturbed?*

He woke up in the morning from a crazy dream, basically re-living yesterday's events.

No school today, luckily. His mother let him sleep through the morning hours and wake up at his own pace.

He did not say a word during breakfast. He

just thought about the Silence some more. He tried to remember the feeling of hearing nothing. He, unsurprisingly, found it difficult. It was not easy for the human mind to imagine something it had only experienced briefly; especially something this novel. The more he tried the more distorted his image would get. The only thing he was sure of was what he felt during the event. It was just like trying to remember a vivid dream.

Mark had always been the type of kid to seek help when he felt he needed it. His parents had both understood that while he was young and were quite fine with letting their child explore on his own. Every time he would ask, they would answer every question as best they could. Mark was a smart kid and they figured the teachers were doing their job.

He had not been too troublesome or rebellious, which was great for his mom and dad, but not too shy either. He had made plenty of friends and had been doing very well in school.

For these reasons, even though she saw he was troubled today, his mum scratched the top of his head when she walked by, and patiently waited for him to come to her for help, if he needed it.

Mark finished his breakfast and got up to put his dirty dishes in the dishwasher, when Dan walked in through the side door of the kitchen.

"Hey Mrs D!"

"Hi, Dan," she answered as she always did, quickly glancing over at him and smiling and then going back again at the cupboard she was putting things in.

"Freaky, huh?" Dan asked, trying in a roundabout way to see if she was doing alright.

"What's that?" she replied, hoping that he was talking about something other than the obvious.

"The 'Silence'," he said, bringing his arms up in front, playfully imitating an animal showing its claws.

"Yeah, that was weird."

To put it lightly she thought, pausing for just half a second.

"So everyone heard that?" she asked rhetorically.

"Yeah, they talked about it on the news this morning. Funny how it's all the states around Wyoming."

"Is it?" Sarah replied, intrigued.

By this point Mark was done putting his dishes away. He looked over at Dan and gestured with his head towards the door leading further inside the house.

"Come on, I've got an idea," he said to him.

"I bet," Dan answered, putting his hands in the pockets of his black track pants and then followed Mark upstairs to his room.

The boys went up the blue carpeted, creaky

wooden stairs and reached Mark's room at the end of the corridor, just above the kitchen.

The silence broke with Dan's question:

"You're still thinking about yesterday, huh?"

Mark sat down at his desk and shimmied off in his chair to the right, spinning to face Dan. On the desk sat the detector he had bought from Radio Shack, with the headphones plugged in, dangling an inch above the floor.

"I plugged these in yesterday and listened for hours."

Dan took a seat on the bed off to the left, facing his friend, legs spread apart and elbows on his knees and leaning forward.

Mark continued:

"At first I thought it was just me, but the signal is constant." He tapped the desk rhythmically, about once every second. "It went on and on and it was getting softer and softer…"

He paused, picked up the earbuds and rolled the chair towards Dan, handing one to him while putting the other one in his own ear.

"What can you hear?" he asked.

Dan put it in his ear and listened, looking off to his left, at nothing in particular, while he focused.

After a second or two he said:

"Nothing."

"That's right," Mark smiled.

He could now go ahead with his mini-presentation. He grabbed a cylindrical device from behind the detector and pulled the headphones out, which made a scratching noise. He then plugged in this new device in place of the headphones and the headphones in the convenient jack on the other side of it. The same scratching noise now preceded a faint, rhythmic beeping that echoed in and out. They could just about hear it.

"There, yeah!" Dan confirmed.

Mark acknowledged his friend with a nod and then gestures with his left index finger for him to wait. He used his other hand to turn a dial on the little device. It was the volume dial. He got about three quarters of the way to full volume and this time it was unmistakable: there was now a relatively loud, rhythmic beeping coming from the detector and through the headphones.

"So, what's this mean, then?" Dan asked, curiously.

Mark briefly explained to Dan that he had walked around the room and even outside last night with the detector and he thought the beeping got louder when he walked in a particular cardinal direction.

"We need to head south," he explained, "before the sound becomes too faint for us to hear."

Dan took out the earbud and handed it over to

Mark.

"To find what?"

"Whatever caused this, man! Don't you wanna know?"

A bit reluctantly and perhaps even a little frightened, Dan replied:

"I dunno, man, what if it's dangerous?"

Mark tried, in his own way to relieve his friend's fear:

"More dangerous than being attacked in broad daylight by zombie dudes? Twice?"

"Well, shit, when you put it that way... I guess you're not wrong...How far do you think it is?"

Mark shrugged and answered as best he could:

"Just outside of town? We can always turn around if something happens," he reassured him.

Convinced, Dan got up from the bed.

"Well, I gotta go tell mom and get my backpack."

Excited, Mark replied:

"Yeah! You do that, I'll strap this to the bike. Meet me back here. I'll be in the garage."

The two nodded in agreement and Dan headed off to let his mum know he would be out for the day. On the way he hyped himself up, saying to himself *this is cool* and reminding himself that every time he had followed Mark into some weird trip or experiment, they had always had fun. And they had always been able to get out of any sticky situations.

Mark took the detector downstairs. On the way, his mother reminded him that she would be out for the day, and to take a set of keys if he wanted to head out.

She was not going to work today; in fact, neither of the Daniels was. Joshua, her husband, was already at the hospital with his father. He had had some sort of condition develop just after the first Silence hit. Not many people were correlating the event with any adverse reactions. So far, many doctors believed it was just a coincidence. Regardless, Sarah was leaving shortly, and she reminded Mark about it. He packed his bags accordingly.

In the garage, he found some rope and tied the detector to the front of his bicycle. He made sure it was safe by pulling slightly in every direction on the device. *I'll notice if it starts to fall off and I'll just stop and fix it*, he thought. *Yeah that's fine*.

In his backpack he made sure to grab extra batteries, his camera – which he charged last night to make sure he could film everything – not one but two bottles of water just in case, and a couple of tools like a screwdriver and pliers. *You never know*.

Waiting for Dan to return, he also thought it

could be useful to pack a couple of snacks and some cash, for emergencies.

Dan cycled back to Mark's house. He had his own backpack with whatever he had thought necessary to bring. It was almost lunch time now, but they had both had a late breakfast; plus they had snacks, so they headed off south down the street, out of Casper.

Mark had one headphone in his ear and the other wrapped around his neck. He had strapped the detector with the dial facing up, so he could adjust the volume. According to the little experiment he had performed the night before, it was going to get louder.

They rode off past the last of the houses. Now they could only see a gas station, some houses under construction, abandoned buildings, a 7/11 and empty lots in-between.

The echoing beeps were getting louder but the rhythm stayed consistent. The boys reached the edge of town and the volume dial was all the way down. The sound however was as loud as it could be; almost unbearably so. They reached an abandoned warehouse; the last building within the town limits.

This must be it, they both thought. Mark wrapped the other earbud around his neck and led Dan towards the open mesh fence gate.

The eerie-looking abandoned warehouse stood menacingly behind a metal fence, inviting them in.

CHAPTER 18

When an exceptional event happens that messes with one's senses, especially as strongly as the Silence has, the border between dream and reality gets slightly blurred. Logic alone might not be enough to discern fact from illusion.

Dr Leopold Smith woke up in the temporary quarters he had been assigned. He did not remember dreaming, but he did slowly begin to recall details about what had happened before he had fallen asleep.

He felt strange; as if he had had a full night's rest. He could not have slept that long, he thought.

He looked around the room not even

knowing why, but he found a clock hanging on the wall. He was rightly surprised to see it showing eight AM.

Before he had a chance to start thinking about anything, his body reminded him of the important things like eating and going to the bathroom. He conceded that he was feeling weak and decided to try to find the mess hall. *Breakfast first, dealing with these idiots next*, he thought.

Slowly but surely more of his brain turned on as he shambled around and stumbled across the mess hall by accident. He did not want to question it so he grabbed his meal and sat down at a table close to the exit, by himself.

He noticed something: the world sounded normal. The voices of all the soldiers having their breakfast and walking around were set against the familiar background of a constant buzzing. An imperceptible ringing that he knew was there but to which his sense of hearing had evolved to ignore, given that this was what had been normal for humans and every other creature for billions of years.

Lost in sluggish thoughts Dr Smith performed a simple act which came natural to everyone but him. Taking care of oneself and responding to one's bodily needs was something that he rarely kept up with. Sleepless nights and strange eating habits were much too common for him. At least when he was home, his loving wife took care of him by demanding that he kept to a schedule. He might not have acted like it around her, but he was very grateful.

Here at the base, however, after a long night at the lab and no breakfast lunch or dinner the day before, he was forced to eat and sleep when his body no longer accepted any input other than the necessary. Having an argument about something he was passionate about, had not helped much either.

The mess hall seemed to have emptied all of a sudden. The odd straggler getting a late breakfast was all that he saw. His tray was almost empty too.

He dipped into his pocket for an aspirin, which he took with the remaining water in the plastic bottle he was given. He looked around and saw used trays all over, being picked up by the staff. He got up to try and find some answers.

The underground maze was still a blur but somehow the flawless design lent itself to easy navigation. Without actually knowing what direction to go, Dr Leopold found his way back to the main chamber where the device that bore his name was being housed.

He entered the room using the same door he was staring through yesterday. He looked around at the other scientists, thinking that they were likely unaware of the possible ramifications of using such a dangerous and highly unpredictable device. Many more studies at much lower power levels had to be done before continuing this risky exercise.

He scanned around for his disesteemed colleague and quickly located him in a nearby room that seemed to be his office.

With the door wide open and behind his desk opposite the entrance to this small study, Dr Kim was skimming some documents and appeared stressed. Leopold did not seem concerned and approached him, standing in the doorway with his arms crossed. He cleared his throat and passive-aggressively tried to get his colleague's attention:

"Dr Kim…"

Surprised and baffled, he lifted his head and paused to figure out why he had just heard Leopold's voice calling out. He had a sheet of paper in each hand which he promptly put down as he got ready to respond.

With feigned confidence he replied by uttering his colleague's name as well.

At that point Leopold started a staring contest with Dr Kim, condescendingly and authoritatively looking straight into his old friend's confused and perhaps even frightened eyes.

After a few seconds pause Dr Kim continued to act ignorant.

"What can I do for you?" he asked, his voice very slightly trembling, trying to ignore the gigantic centrepiece problem in the room behind Leopold.

"Care to explain?" Leo asked, keeping his no bullshit tone.

Exhaling once and smiling as if to pretend

there was no issue whatsoever, his former colleague replied:

"Explain what?"

By that point the energy from his hearty breakfast had already started to kick in. He managed to find it within himself to not completely bite Dr Kim's head off.

"Don't play games," he said, matching his colleague's fake smile.

Dr Kim's mind was racing. *Should I lie to him? What would be the point now...What do I tell him? He knows I stole his work...*

He began with a very long "I" but in his head his thoughts screamed at him: *am screwed...what the HELL do I tell him?!*

Leopold gave him ample time to finish his barely begun sentence; so much so that the silence in-between his words was beginning to become awkward. Dr Kim gestured with his hands as if showing him something but he still had not said a second word yet.

Keeping with his passive-aggressive tone but clearly attempting to give his former friend the benefit of the doubt, however pointless that may have be, Leo matched the length of the pronoun but actually made a sentence follow:

"You...stole my work."

He crossed his arms and continued:

"But why?"

Between each question he gave Dr Kim a moment to reflect.

"What made you betray me?" his face showed disgust as he utters that word

"What made you think it was appropriate to sell off something that's not yours?"

There was no answer there that would satisfy him. The reality that they both knew was that it had been greed and selfishness that had caused it. But it was coming to terms with that, and apologising that Dr Kim found difficult; almost impossible.

"I just want to understand…" he trailed off.

This time the pause was a bit longer. Leopold's eyes now looked at his old colleague and friend not with disgust and disdain, but with pity.

After a brief moment of self-reflection, following a long time of doubt since the moment he had made that first step in betraying his colleague, Dr Kim decided to answer truthfully:

"We needed the money; and—"

Appalled at the notion, Leopold interrupted him:

"Money?" he raised his voice. "And who's 'we'?"

"Look, you don't understand—" Dr Kim quickly jumped back in.

"What don't I understand? That—"

Before he could finish his potentially harmful comment, their discussion that would have soon turned into a heated argument was cut short by general Warfield, joined by his posse:

"Dr Kim!" he yelled.

His shout resonated across both rooms.

"Where are we with phase two?"

Alarm bells started going off in Leopold's head and he chipped in surprised (even though he really should not have been) that his warnings had not been heeded at all:

"Hold on, phase two? Wha—"

He got interrupted again, as if he had just turned invisible, this time by Dr Kim who answered the general reluctantly.

"I need a bit more time," he said to the general, with a tone that seemed to ask for forgiveness from his old friend as he looked Leopold in his eyes.

"You've got until noon." the General told him. He turned to walk away and continued talking:

"We've poured a lot of money into this, and the higher-ups are liking the results."

Dr Smith was in awe, his jaw as far down as it could go. Before he got a chance to make sure his colleague was not serious about going forward with any more activations, Dr Kim took charge of the conversation. He looked at him apologetically:

"I'm sorry. My hands are tied—"

"You're not serious about this…" Leo pleaded.

"Stay and help me!" Dr Kim said with hopeful eyes.

"Help you what?" said Leo, grounding the conversation. "Destroy the country? Kill people?"

Deluded beyond belief, Dr Kim denied the seriousness of the issue and invited his former colleague again to stay and help.

Without a warning or any obvious reason Leopold stormed off with his head in his hands muttering "unbelievable…"

Behind him, Dr Kim sighed and returned to his work, getting up to close the door, looking with regret at his old friend leaving, before sitting back down.

The signs guided a driven Leopold to the exit of the bunker. Once out, he called a taxi and gave the driver the address for his old lab outside of town. He wanted to take the matter into his own hands. *Someone has to stop these fools before they do something   stupid.*

CHAPTER 19

With their main lead sitting comfortably in interrogation room two, detectives Miller and Simmons were preparing their strategy. They were not even sure what exactly they were looking to get out of this guy but he would definitely spill something. They all did eventually. Hopefully, among all the lies he might say, they could find something to go on.

At the very least they needed to get to the bottom of what had happened the day before.

A variation on good cop - bad cop struck their fancy. Old reliable rarely failed to get at least some results.

The suspects did not have to say anything. In fact, they had the right to remain silent because anything they said to the police could and would be used against them in court; but that did not mean a detective or officer could not just sit in an interrogation room with them and ask questions. The problem with the human mind in a questioning situation is that it cannot help itself; people always talk. And if they talked, they were sure to give away something.

Psychology plays a big role in interrogations and these tactics are not illegal. No one is forcing anyone to talk; not physically anyway. Some might argue it is immoral to use psychology as a weapon, but humanity is not that civilised yet.

After letting the man sweat in uncomfortable silence for almost two hours, the two slowly entered the room.

Besides the strategic move of letting boredom and all sorts of thoughts creep into the suspect's head, the detectives had used this time to gather up as much information on the man as possible.

Michael Vincent was the man they had grabbed earlier just because they had probable cause. Too many times arrests were made with only that as a motive, but the psychology of each suspect was such that a cause could always be thought up. In their subconscious, they knew they were guilty; there had to be a good reason, otherwise why were they running? And this thinking would lead to their downfall.

The two had also managed to get a bit more about Michael's personal life: his ex-girlfriend, his unpaid debts, his dead parents; things they would slowly bring up as time went by to put him off balance and make him slip up.

Richard walked in first.

"Hey Mike," he began with a friendly tone. "I'm really sorry to keep you waiting. I'm detective Simmons, this is my partner detective Miller," he pointed in his partner's general direction, "he's here to…" he paused to help make the joke land better, "stand there and watch like a creep."

He smiled to hammer the joke in.

As he sat down, he swiftly continued his next sentence with almost no gap in-between:

"Before we start, I need to make sure you're aware, you must be, you look like a clever man…" he made a millisecond pause and then repeated himself on purpose, "I need to make sure you know your rights."

He proceeded to read him his Miranda rights and ask him to verbally confirm he had understood; a simple request, really, but clearly one with hidden meaning. Once the silent Mike opened his mouth, that was Richard's foot in the door.

Detective Simmons calmly explained to suspect Mike that he needed to confirm. In fact Mike did not need to say or do anything apart from request a lawyer, but that did not cross his mind. Either his ego or boredom got the better of Michael because he reluctantly answered under his breath. At that point, it was all downhill for him. He got asked again to confirm because the detective "didn't hear" him. He needed to make sure the man understood his rights; or at least that was what he told Mike.

What followed was a slow, methodical mind game between the three, with James only being a part of it through his presence. Every once in a while suspect Mike looked up at him uncomfortably. No matter how friendly the discussion seemed between Richard and Mike, James's daunting stare from next to the door would put him on edge.

The direct approach almost never worked. Suspects would rarely speak directly about the thing they had done (or thought they had done). But a carefully planned discussion, seemingly beating around the bush or even sometimes going down a completely unrelated path, would always give the interrogators some piece of information that they could later put together. It was all a puzzle they were trying to solve and it was all on camera for later analysis.

After two long, arduous hours of constant psychological barrage from the good cop, Mike could not keep his stories straight. He had been trying his damnedest not to lie too much and also not to reveal something the detectives did not already know.

Their interrogation led them down the path of

trying to piece together what the purpose of the M-M detector was.

"If you invert the sound," Mike reluctantly told, "some people put the headphones on and it helps them have a safe, mellow trip, you know? So I've heard," he said attempting to make it seem like he was just speculating.

At that point, however, the detectives knew he knew, and in the back of his mind, Mike knew they knew, but was just denying it to himself. Maybe the fact that the tone of the conversation was so light and unrelated meant they just wanted information. He had not done anything. He had just run. *Yeah, that's it. They'll let me go after this*, he lied to himself.

"So where would they get the headphones from?" Richard asked still with a friendly but no-BS tone.

"There's this guy down in Regis." Mike conceded.

This is when he made himself think he was given them something to go on, so they would repay him by letting him go. They of course have no obligation or intention to do so.

"Where in Regis?" Richard inquired. "Can you give me an address?"

Mike picked up the pen and piece of paper that detective Simmons handed him and scribbled down an address in the Regis neighbourhood of

Denver.

"Am I free to go now?" Mike asked, with hopeful eyes?

"Yeah," Richard disingenuously reassured him, "as soon as we check this out make sure it's legit. You just hang tight."

He smiled and got up from the table, exhausted but not showing it, and gestured with his head to his partner to leave the room.

They had the dealer and one of his accomplices now, if the address was solid.

From their long discussion they had gathered that Michael appeared to be working alone. They could send someone to search his tent under the bridge and the two could investigate this address in north-west Denver.

The two waited to get a bit further away from the interrogation room before discussing any plans, just to be safe. On their way out of the hallway, as they crossed the threshold into the main cubicle area of the precinct, another detective stopped Richard to let him know the news she had heard. She was in a hurry to get to the other side of the building so she told him to look up news from Casper; the town where his nephew, Daniel lived. He yelled after her to find out more but she was already halfway down the corridor they had just come out of. He pulled up his phone and searched for Casper news. Key words jumped out at him and he got a bit apprehensive. People injured, drug addicts on a rampage, something about local children, the Silence. His mind was racing. He called his sister Kelly to check up on them. They were fine. Dan had been out with his friend all day and now he was in his room playing video games.

With his mind at ease he told his partner that it had been too long of a shift. They both agreed to call it a day and check the address the next day. They sent someone to finish processing suspect Mike and each headed home to get a good sleep. They also needed to process everything that had happened and get their thoughts in order.

The entire way out of the building the two walked together. Their desks were relatively close to one another and they both needed to pick up some stuff, arrange their paperwork and turn off their work computers. Their lockers were also side by side, and both their cars were parked one space over in the underground parking lot of the precinct.

Their eyes never meet and they did not exchange any words, not even a "see you tomorrow" like they always told each other. They were both contemplating.

The mind of detective Simmons was racing from one topic to another: the Silence, his nephew, the victim, the connection (or lack thereof) between everything. Did those drug dealers have anything to do with the Silence? Was it all a coincidence?

He was home now. For some inexplicable reason he felt apprehensive again; this time for tomorrow. Should they even go to that address? Was it a trap? The maps application on his phone read it was just a residential address.

His wife could not get a single word out of him. He fell asleep in silence after a quiet dinner.

Detective Miller's mind was different in the way that it worked, but he was having the same thoughts.

His main concern was with the overwhelming truth of reality. *Was it just an illusion? So Silent...*

He got to listen to the radio in his car on the way back home. They mentioned something about how many states were affected: *a radius around Wyoming? Isn't that where Richard's sister lives?* he tried to remember.

He went out late to walk Archie, his brown spotted white beagle, like he always did. He used this time to think and smoke outside his apartment. He fell asleep watching TV like always, Archie by his side. Later on in the night he moved to his bed but he very rarely remembered having done so.

The two detectives had a similar dream that night, all sparked by their experiences of the day before; some variation of going to a new address to investigate a tip from someone and being ambushed. First, the Silence hit. Headaches struck violently and in less than a second they were being jumped by a handful of people frothing at the mouth. They tried to pull their guns out but there was no time to aim.

They ran. They reached an abandoned factory with a mesh fence. They went inside and seemed to have escaped. They wandered through the maze-like corridors aimlessly for what felt like hours until they reached a metal security door. They pushed it open. Inside, in the very centre of the tall featureless room, there stood an imposing machine humming and vibrating. It was quiet. Not just regular quiet but Silent. Their minds could not fully recreate the sensation of the Silence but the emotion was the same. From a moment of awe they were pushed into a moment of fear; literally. The frothing maniacs had found them and begun eating them alive as they each woke up in a cold sweat in the morning just before their alarms.

Mrs Simmons was already awake and had had some breakfast and coffee ready. Richard said good morning to her and they discussed the events of the day before. Whatever it was, they were OK and that was what mattered. She forgave him for ignoring her the night before.

Archie was hungry. James made himself a coffee and filled his bowl. It was too early for him to have breakfast though.

He walked around looking for something but found something else: the mess Archie must have made the day before; *or in the night?* he thought. He would have heard it. Archie never made a mess. He was a very good boy.

James cleaned it up nonetheless and got ready to leave. He gave Archie the regular goodbye hug and kiss and headed out.

With the events of their dreams forgotten and a renewed desire to get to the bottom of things, the two detectives drove to work where they had their daily briefings. They did not pay too much attention; most of the things that were said did not concern them or their department, but they had to be there.

They finished their coffee, grabbed the usual gear and walked downstairs to the parking lot.

Their silver, unmarked police cruiser was sitting in the lot, waiting to go on its next mission.

The two barely said a word to each other. Not even James's usual morning joke about "the only loyal employee," talking about the cruiser. Had they greeted each other? They could not remember. *It would be too awkward now*, they thought.

Richard was behind the wheel.

"What's the address again?" he broke the ice.

His partner gave him a zip code which detective Simmons entered into the GPS.

"What do you think we're gonna find?" he asked his more experienced colleague.

After a momentary pause, detective Miller replied:

"I don't know, but for some reason I think we need to keep our guns handy."

Richard looked at him briefly while driving out of the parking lot and after a small pause of his own he said:

"Yeah, I know what you mean."

It felt like forever this time around to get to their destination. The address was all the way in the North-West corner of Denver. Luckily morning traffic was going the other way. There was also the added benefit of having regular silence; the kind that allowed them to think. Although by the looks of Richard's arms and hands tightening around the steering wheel that might not have been a good thing.

About what felt like halfway through the journey, James asked his partner:

"What are you thinking?"

"I don't know what it is..." he answered, looking around not just for the sake of driving safely, but also for his own survival. He was on edge. "Might be the dream last night..." he sighed.

The soft female voice of the GPS reminded them that after a right hand turn they would soon arrive at their destination. Their perception of time was clearly warped by everything that's on both of their minds.

"We'll talk about it later," said Richard. After all, he had had a similarly unsettling dream as well.

They parked up across from the house they needed to visit.

It had no fence, a lawn that had not been

tended to in weeks, it looked like, and a very suspiciously looking heavy door to an otherwise normal-looking suburban house.

The two released their pistols from their holsters and unbuttoned their jackets. They looked around and assessed the area before they exited the car. A skinny shirtless man was mowing the lawn in the same back and forth direction in front of the house next door, on the right hand side. On the left, a blonde woman was doing some gardening. They could not figure out why they were they getting more on edge the longer they waited.

They looked to their right, on their side of the street across from the suspicious house. Nothing.

No cars driving on the road either.

It was quiet.

While opening the door, detective Miller said to his partner:

"We're gonna have to go at some point."

Detective Simmons followed suit and they both stepped out.

Richard locked the car and they both walked towards the house, crossing eyes as they looked out for cars.

As they approached the door, the lawnmower that had been humming in the background stopped running. It did not sound like it was out of fuel though.

Before James got to knock, they heard a muffled thud inside.

He knocked three times on the metal door. It sounded hollow. The sound echoed inside the house. They could not hear anything else.

A few seconds of no-one answering made Richard curious. He looked in through the window on the left hand side. The curtains were drawn, however, and he could not spot any motion. He thought he spotted movement.

As he turned around to inform his partner, a wave of Silence washed over them. It was different this time. It was more like a series of waves of the Loudness of everyday life and the Silence they had experienced twice so far. Perhaps their bodies were used to the feeling or the pain because there was no headache this time; just the momentary confusion.

Richard, fully turned around, had a split second to warn James of the approaching danger: frothing at the mouth and with his skinny arms flailing in the air, the man who had been mowing the lawn earlier was now rushing detective Miller while his back was turned.

Richard pushed James out of the way and they both fell on the overgrown concrete pathway leading to the house.

The maniac was now on the floor as well, having run diagonally, full force into the heavy door. It did not take him long to get up however, and he was looking for his target again, aiming to finish whatever his attack had been.

By the time the two got up on their feet and started running for the car, but before the initial attacker managed to recover, the woman they had spotted gardening earlier was also up and had the same crazed look in her eyes.

The waves of Silence got stronger and stronger, and they followed one another more frequently. Silence, reality. Silence, reality. Over and over. Faster and faster.

They bolted for the car. Out of the house across the street, behind their car, they saw, and most definitely heard, a couple fighting.

James went around the car to the passenger side and Richard looked for the key in his pocket. They both got in at the same time and slammed the doors in unison.

"Get us out of here!" James yelled as his partner was staring out the window at the approaching maniacs.

By now the waves seemed to have cancelled each other out. Somehow though, they could still hear something...off about the world. It was as if the volume of the ringing in their ears, the one that people were only aware of when it was gone, had been turned down even further. The background sounded even more muffled now; even more Silent.

They pulled over on the side of the road once it was safe to do so. They each took a deep breath, occasionally looking back and around the vehicle to make sure it was.

"What the HELL was that?" Richard asked loudly, but without raising his voice, as the two took a moment to process their next move.

CHAPTER 20

At the supposed abandoned lab in Casper the boys reached the gate of the supposed source, or at least one of them, of the beeping Mark had found embedded in the signal he had picked up last night. They parked up their bikes on the side of the mesh enclosure and went to investigate.

The padlock and chain were hanging on the wide open gate. *Abandoned or not, someone must be inside*, the boys thought. Mark grabbed his detector setup from his bike and gestured to his buddy to follow him in. As they entered the large empty lot in front of the warehouse-looking laboratory with only small windows just under the roof, a car pulled up and parked just in front of the bikes. From inside her red two-door sports car, Nancy Phillips was trying to determine if she was in the right place; and why two teenagers were walking up to the door of this lab; if she was even in the right place.

The boys ignored the car as they had not yet figured out it was here for the same reason they were.

Mark guided Dan to the front door of the metal building, past some old broken pallets from underneath which rats looked on. At that point he only had one headphone close to his ear. The volume was at minimum and it was still overwhelming. He shut it off. He was sure they were in the right place.

Nancy was still unsure but she got out of her car nonetheless. *This doesn't look like a lab to me,* she thought.

She noticed the two snooping around the main doors and decided to approach carefully.

She put on the "adult face" and confronted the boys who looked like they were trying to figure out how to get in.

"Hey," she yelled just loudly enough for them to hear her from across the front yard. "Are you supposed to be here?"

Mark, without hesitation retorted with the volume of his voice matching hers:

"Are you?"

Well shit, they got me there, Nancy thought.

Thinking on her feet she replied:

"Yes. I'm looking for the lab of Dr Rogers." She said coming closer so as not to have to yell.

The boys' minds started racing as more puzzle pieces started coming in.

"Is he the one who caused the Silence?" Mark intelligently asked.

"No," Nancy continued as she got closer. She did not want to have to keep shouting. "He thinks this might be where it all started though. What do you know about the Silence?"

Mark and Dan looked at each other as if to determine between themselves if she was trustworthy enough to be included in their investigation.

"Listen to this."

Mark handed her an earbud and instructed her not to put it in her ear but to hold it close.

The loud, high-pitched rhythmic pinging took her by surprise, as Mark turned his contraption on. He left it playing for a few seconds and then shut it back off.

"What is that?" Nancy asked.

"Some sort of echo," Mark explained while also trying to make sense of it himself, "from whatever was used to make everything Silent. The device has to be in here."

He looked up and around still trying to figure

out how to get in.

Completely unbothered and nonchalantly Nancy reached for the metal door handle on the shiny warehouse entrance and pushed it open.

"Huh" the boys exclaimed softly in unison.

Nancy took the lead and opened the door all the way letting the bright sun shine in through the metal entrance, adding to the ambient light flowing in through the small, dusty, high windows.

They all walked into the eerie, empty warehouse and were intrigued by the centrepiece: a large mechanical construction encased in glass from ceiling to floor with pipes, wires, glass tubes, buttons, dials and valves all around. To its left and right two sets of consoles with glowing lights and flashing screens. On the opposite side of this magnificent device sat shelves containing a plethora of books, tools and other small machinery all strewn about with no evident rhyme or reason behind their placement.

The three introduced themselves and began carefully looking for any clues as to what was going on. The flashing screens displayed unintelligible error messages and failure notices. Engrossed in their search, none of them heard the faint sound of car tyres on gravel as Dr Smith's taxi dropped him off behind Nancy's car.

Perplexed as to why two bicycles and a microcar would be parked out front of his old lab, Leopold confidently walked in through the open door, left this way by the three intruders, and approached them.

His anger and frustration had dissipated on the drive over so now he talked with a curious tone rather than a confrontational one.

"Hello? Can I help you?"

Confidently yet still wrongfully Mark himself interrogated the strange man at the door.

"Who are you?"

Taken aback by the audacity of this "*punk*", Leopold raised both his eyebrows and with a single guffaw he flipped the question onto him:

"I should ask you the same thing, young man. What are you doing in MY lab?"

Hearing this, Nancy de-escalated:

"Hi, my name is Nancy Phillips. I'm a friend of Dr Rogers'."

The man seemed to be accepting of her explanation and allowed her to continue, displaying interest without saying a word.

She continued:

"He's in—" she paused and corrected herself "he WAS in a coma in Denver but the Silence woke him up." *That sounds so dumb*, she thought.

This intrigued Leopold and his demeanour was now solidly curious.

They exchanged names and stories. Nancy

recounted her shift yesterday, focusing on the important details like when she had witnessed Renfrew awaken from his three year coma, and the discussion she had had (what she remembered of it anyway) with the two doctors in the research labs. She also mentioned the reaction of the man restrained to the hospital bed that Dr Nowell had sedated and the stories she had heard about other patients, druggies, reacting the same, seemingly because of the Silence.

The boys described their experiment, eager and excited to talk to a fellow scientist. Leopold was surprised at Mark's ingenuity when it came to finding this place. They both realised a bit of luck had been involved, but that did not mean he did not perform some good experiments and detective work.

Dr Smith, as the good teacher that he was, described in enough detail – not too much as to overload his audience's minds – how his invention worked. This captivated Mark, intrigued Dan enough to listen (but it was unsure how much he would actually remember after the fact) and all Nancy cared about was getting back to Mr Rogers with as much information as she could.

It fascinated them how the Silence affected different people; each, of course, being interested for different reasons. *It would be quite interesting and scary if this effect were global*, they all thought.

EPISODE 6

CHAPTER 21

Dr Kim had managed to convince himself he was not an evil man. *If only they knew the whole story*, he thought. He was a respected scientist and to those who had had the pleasure to know him he was a decent friend. No one is perfect and he did not claim to be.

He had certainly made mistakes; some of which had come to bite him in the behind. More recently, his betrayal of his fellow doctor (and most likely former friend) Dr Leopold Smith.

Confronted with the reality of his situation, behind a desk in a windowless room, in an underground military bunker doing research for the army, using ideas he had stolen and sold, Dr Kim pondered; not on his past mistakes, of which he had made many; not of the ramifications of "his" research, but of how he could make it up to his friend.

Col. Danski entered his barely lit office and found Dr Kim with his head rather literally buried in paperwork.

He cleared his throat and called out softly:

"Dr Kim?"

The muffled voice of a troubled man replied:

"Yes?"

"Your appointment with the general?" the colonel reminded him.

"Tell him I'll be right there," Richard said, still not lifting his head up from his desk.

"Understood," the colonel said and exited, closing the door behind him.

After one more long and arduous minute Richard awakened, still debating the dilemma he was now faced with: shut it all down and commit career suicide, but in the process potentially make it up to his former friend and even help, or double down on his mistake and walk in shame with money in hand and the adoration of his employers, knowing that he had probably helped start World War Three...

The choice seemed easy on paper but the difficulty lay in its execution. Real life is almost always slightly more complicated than black and white.

He walked out of his office empty-handed. He closed the door gently and started his own personal a walk of shame through the big room housing the element of his frustrations. On the way, he pondered the dilemma some more until the very last second he entered the meeting room.

At the meeting, to which he was now fifteen minutes late, he was confronted with something that was certainly not making things easier: the military wanted to take the project to its next step already; way ahead of schedule. They wanted more power, a larger scale and, in the not too distant future, potential offshore deployment.

No amount of pleas for reconsideration or reminders and advice that the data would need to be thoroughly analysed before proceeding were able to convince the general. An argument erupted between the two, but according to his boss plans had already been set in motion.

"You're either with us or you can find your own way out my bunker," general Warfield authoritatively dictated.

Silence erupted in this small room overlooking his abominable re-creation.

Dr Kim stared at it and he made his own decision silently. It was high time he started taking charge of his own fate. He politely informed the general of his resignation effective immediately. The general was disappointed but not entirely surprised.

"I knew it would be too much for you Dr" he mocked.

Two officers escorted him out of the meeting room and back into his makeshift office. He packed whatever belongings he felt he needed and even managed to grab some plans and schematics that, should anyone have found out he was taking, would certainly have got him in a lot of trouble. Luckily the two young privates were completely oblivious to the doctor's actions and even if they had suspected anything, they would not be able to tell the difference between power consumption statistics or operating instructions and tax reports; it was all paperwork to them and they had been ordered to be polite.

On their way out the general returned and cut them off in the main chamber, the Leopold device looming to the general's left hand side. Dr Kim, knowing he had got hold of sensitive documentation that could land him in Guantanamo Bay, he thought, tried his best to remain calm but still grasped at his briefcase with his other hand.

The general, not saying a word and with the same stoic look on his face, reached his hand out towards him. The doctor stared and hid his horror. *This is it*, he thinks.

"I'd like to apologise," the general told him.

Confused and still on edge, Dr Kim asked what for.

"For the way I treated you in there," he

continued. "It's your choice to leave, and I respect that. You've been a great asset and a man of honour and integrity on this project and it is a great loss to see you leave."

With a slight stutter the doctor thanked him and shook the general's hand, letting go of the briefcase with his right hand and attempting to act as normal as possible.

They said goodbye with a look and a nod and the doctor and his escort walked off, but not before the general reminded him of the non-disclosure agreement he had signed when he had joined.

Relieved but also still on edge, the doctor walked to the lift. Every corner he and his escort took, he thought was going to be the last; that they would catch him. He was waiting for the colonel's voice to call out to him.

Thankfully, he managed to get out and in his car saying goodbye to the two privates who were completely unaware of what had just transpired.

Richard squeezed the steering wheel as hard as he could with his sweaty hands, occasionally wiping some sweat off his forehead. He drove towards Leopold's old lab. *That's where he must've gone,* he thought.

At the lab, the doctor was giving Nancy and the boys a crash course on how to use some of the consoles and monitoring devices around the Leopold Device. It was relatively easy to operate any one system and report readings even though a user might not have understood the full picture.

After Mark had shown Dr Smith his own findings and had got him up to speed on his and Dan's journey, Leopold had become worried.

"Whatever they did," he said, "must've made quite the ripple on the Luminiferous Aether; and ironically this lab isn't equipped to measure changes in the aether to such a fine degree."

After listening again to the loud high-pitched ringing playing in Mark's headphones, he was determined that the rippling must have been of such a high frequency that any attempt to measure the aetherian waves would be pointless there. He had not installed equipment that sensitive.

A short time later after this realization, however, another car pulled up to the entrance of the lab, through the open mesh gates. Through the closed door walked none other than Dr Kim himself. After a brief exchange of looks ranging from "what the hell are you doing here" to "I forgive you because I know why you're here alone," Richard broke the brief silence between them.

"I'm here to help. We have to stop them."

"So you've finally come around then," Leo replied. "Better late than never, I suppose."

Richard approached and brought forward the documents he had "borrowed."

"I think this will help," he said apologetically.

While Leo looked over the plans, Nancy introduced herself and the boys and Dr Kim replied in kind.

Dan, without a second's thought, called him out:

"So you're the guy that stole Dr Smith's work!"

Everyone except Leo looked at Dan in slight awe of this display of courage.

Richard bowed his head a bit and confirmed it was indeed him that had caused the mess.

"But I'm here to help fix it. That's gotta be worth something," he pleaded.

With his eyes still glued to the paper and seemingly oblivious to what was going on around him, Leo appeared to answer his question:

"Yes, yes; this could work."

He flipped some pages and headed over to a couple of consoles to type some things into the computer. For a few seconds the others stood around in awkward silence. A minute or two into his reprogramming he lifted his head and looked at the others with a smile informing them of his success:

"That should do it," he said.

"That should do what, sir?" Mark curiously asked, moving closer.

Dr Smith explained, reminding him of their previous conversation about the lack of sensitivity in the sensors in this lab, that now that he had the plans to their version of his device, he could calibrate it better to the power levels they are using, which would hopefully allow them to counteract, "maybe even completely stop their attempts at bringing about this Silence, whatever their motivation is."

With renewed enthusiasm, Leo briefly explained to everyone what he was trying to do and gave everyone a task.

Knowing the specifications for their apparatus he could extrapolate what inputs to give his device here so that hopefully they would nullify the Silence when it inevitably fell again.

They all moved to their respective consoles, Mark and Dan on the right-hand side monitoring power, Nancy and Dr Kim on the left keeping an eye on output levels, and Leopold in the centre, controlling it all. They took a seat on some old metal folding chairs that were hidden in one of the corners of the warehouse under some old boxes, and prepared for power-up. From what Richard had told them, they did not have much time until the army proceeded with their next, larger scale activation.

Consulting with Richard, Leo decided to wait until they activated theirs. It was potentially safer than trying to anticipate the signal.

An uncomfortably long amount of time passed before that happened though. It seemed like hours, but they had to be prepared. None of them let themselves get too lost in thought. They stayed quiet.

Ready or not however, the Silence was harrowing. They blinked and it was as if they had just woken up from a life-long dream into another dream, also incredibly vivid and real. They knew both were real, but they could not shake the feeling of something being off about both.

But this time they did not have much time to dwell. As soon as the ringing in their ears stopped and the colours shifted, they got to work. Everything was set so that only Leo had to initiate the sequence and the rest of them would monitor and report.

As they did, the realisation slowly kicked in: first on Leo's face, because he was the one who understood all the data, and then Richard's. As their brains perceived rhythmic Silence cutting in and out, at first starting about once every second and then faster and faster until it all became one solidly Silent background, their sense that something had gone terribly wrong worsened.

The two doctors shared their dread as the Silence amplified. Just when they all thought they were aware of what reality truly sounded like, the impossible happened: no one could have figured it could get MORE Silent; but then again, no one ever had figured regular silence wasn't as quiet as things could get in the first place. Quieter than being deep in a forest hearing only the breeze in the leaves and the occasional bird chirping; quieter than a meditation room with nothing but the sound of your breath, taking in the smell of scented candles, quieter than the night after you've just put the baby to bed and you fell asleep as if on a bed of clouds.

With a pale visage and a trembling voice Richard explained the gravity of what had just occurred. The effect was now global. The two devices, rather than cancel each other out, had built upon each other's interference with the Aether amplifying a normally, relatively local event. It was possible the effect even reached beyond the Earth.

All they managed to do was stare blankly into the room and in each other's direction and think in unison: *what have we done…*

CHAPTER 22

Detectives James Miller and Richard Simmons were still parked on the side of the road, a safe distance away from the address suspect Mike had given them. To them it felt like they had been sitting there for a good half hour. In Silence. By now the effect had settled into an even deeper stillness than before which the two had not take notice of. They were on edge.

James opened his mouth and took a breath, ready to discuss their next move.

A loud explosion coming from the direction they had left from cut him off though. It sounded as though it happened only a few feet away, like a lightning strike hitting the tree they were parked under.

This boom however was a fair distance away. It had not broken any windows near their car. Its loudness was only amplified by the Silence looming over everything again, this time more ominous than before.

"Was that the place we were just at?" Richard said, turning around in his seat to look in the direction of the detonation.

"I'll call it in," his partner replied, "get us back there...and have your gun ready."

They carefully drove back over in the direction of the black smoke rising up viciously; all the while James was calling for an ambulance and the fire department. They parked some distance away.

The detectives were the first on scene. The two maniacs who had attacked them were lying on the ground among rubble of the house from which James and Richard had driven away at speed.

The heavy metal door now rested in the parking spot they had used, across the street.

Neighbours who had not left for work yet were now outside gawking and filming. An angry old man was yelling loudly, even more so now, because his house had been hit by debris.

In the distance the fire and ambulance sirens could be heard getting closer. In this Silence though, they were still halfway across town.

Out of curiosity and impatience the detectives approached the smoking rubble of the former dwelling. Most of what was floating in the air now was dust from the rubble; the smoke had fully lifted.

Their first sweep on foot of the destroyed home revealed nothing much besides a lack of any visible trace of bodies. *He probably wanted to cover his tracks*, they thought.

The sirens got louder and louder until they had become unbearable. When they made it on scene outside they were turned off.

In the rainbow of colours showering what was left of the walls of this safehouse, the two detectives emerged out of the rubble to explain to the fire-fighters and paramedics what they thought had happened. The fire department quickly and professionally took over the investigation.

A good few hours of waiting and theorising later, the fire-fighters had their preliminary report which they shared with James and Richard, who had stood and watched with anticipation. Later on, they said, they would forward a comprehensive copy.

For now, it looked like an explosion occurred; no one was surprise there. The interesting part was that it had been planned; long before it happened.

The house had been rigged to blow, most

likely as a means to hide evidence, the two postulated. Various bits of cabling and improvised explosive casings were dotted around the premises.

No bodies in the rubble.

After the fire department finished up, all that was left was to catalogue everything; long hours lay ahead for the detectives.

What they found did not so much surprise them as confuse them even further. It seemed the explosion had not destroyed as much as the suspect had wanted.

Large enough quantities of drugs had been left over, mainly heroin, to paint a clear enough picture of what this guy had been doing in his mini-fortress. However, what muddied everything back up were the files they had found on a hard drive hidden away in a fireproof box.

After carefully reading them, in a Silence that made their thoughts sound like they were spoken aloud, they discovered that, whatever that event was, it had happened before; besides the now three other happenings.

Some documents, dating back to a few years prior, mentioned some money transfers from a company called SecuTech. Not a particularly interesting fact on its own. However further documentation existed on the hard drive, carefully sorted in folders as if made for someone to find. A trail of transfers and bills linked the company with a certain Colonel Danski of the US army.

More documents mentioned the use of an "LD-01" device and the purchase of "artificial snow" from an independent contractor called Jamal Davis; also the legal owner of the blown-up house.

The files did not mention anything about the suspect's purchase of Michelson-Morley detectors, however.

After a long day of shock, boring paperwork and maddening Silence, the two turned in for the day, with the hope that they would be able to close the case soon.

At home, each of the two went about their evening routine like normal. James tried to take Archie for a walk, but he was acting out of character. He had knocked over another plant pot and was now laying in the mess he had made, looking up with apologetic eyes. They just stayed together for a bit and James fed him there. Luckily he ate, pausing every time he took a mouthful of dog food and then every other bite. "I can't imagine how your sensitive hearing must be affected when everything is so Silent," James told him softly. They did not go for their usual walk; instead they both sat and watched the news together until they fell asleep.

Richard rang his sister again to check up on her and his nephew. They were all fine. She had just come back from work and Dan had returned from a day-long adventure with his friend Mark. He seemed troubled, but he was doing well. She said she would speak to him some more the next day.

Detective Simmons also sat down to watch the news at eight PM.

This latest event, which had not ended since they were at the house earlier that day, and which inexplicably seemed stronger than its two previous iterations to the inhabitants of the states around Wyoming, the news anchors said was global.

Countries from all around the planet were reporting hearing true Silence for the first time and only now did the rest of the world hear about these events in the United States. No one knew yet the extent of the disruption. This was certainly a case that the two intrepid detectives had only scratched the surface of; a fact which dawned on them as they closed their eyes and began dreaming loudly.

ABOUT THE AUTHOR

Eduard Simion was born and raised in Romania and has lived in the United States, France and currently in the United Kingdom. Growing up he was always fascinated with foreign languages, especially English, and has pursued studies in translation and interpreting in which he was awarded a Master's Degree. Eduard enjoys astronomy and science-fiction and ever since he discovered tabletop role-playing games, he has been absorbed by writing. *The Time the Silence Fell* is his first published story.

Printed in Great Britain
by Amazon